Hear the Screams of the Butterfly
by Troy Camplin

Transcendent Zero Press
Houston, Texas

Copyright © 2016, Troy Camplin

Transcendent Zero Press
www.transcendentzeropress.org

All rights reserved. No part or parts of this book may be reproduced in any format without the expressed written consent of Transcendent Zero Press, or of the author Troy Camplin.

ISBN-13: 978-0692640043
ISBN-10: 0692640045

Library of Congress Control Number: 2016933022

Printed in the United States of America

Transcendent Zero Press
16429 El Camino Real Apt. 7
Houston, TX 77062

Cover design by Glynn Monroe Irby
Cover Model: Cheyenne Henslee

FIRST EDITION

Hear the Screams of the Butterfly
by Troy Camplin

Transcendent Zero Press

Houston, Texas

Table of Contents

Foreword..pages 5-8

Book 1..pages 9-33

Book 2..pages 35-52

Book 3..pages 53-70

Book 4..pages 71-95

Book 5..pages 97-111

About the Author..................................page 113

Foreword

The past year has been difficult. Not for me. For Patric. I had a hard time understanding what was happening to my friend, why he began acting irrational, distant, moody, hostile in a passive-aggressive way until, suddenly, he snapped.

Although I am his closest friend – since grade school – Patric has always been a mystery to me. He was so private, no one knew he had any problems – his friends and I thought Patric was simply becoming more like himself, though in the worst way possible.

I realize now why none of us knew Patric. He buried everything. Patric, the pathological truth-teller, could not live the truth. But you can only bury your problems for so long before something has to give. And something did. Unfortunately, it was Patric's self-control – the most ironic thing he could lose.

Patric was a control freak – not over others, since he's very antiauthoritarian, but over himself. Over circumstances. He had to control everything. He didn't understand that the world is beyond any one person's control, that in order to survive, you have to let things go, accept the world, warts and all. Nor did he understand that just because he could not control the world, that did not mean he could not affect it, even if it was in ways he would never see or fully understand. Maybe his mind decided to show him he was wrong, that he could not always control his life – only something short-circuited and Patric's mind and body became stuck. It's a shame to see such a brilliant mind reduced to mindless rocking in a mental hospital.

That is why I compiled this book. I convinced Patric to write down everything that happened, hoping he would open up so he could get better. I admit, making his problems public is a radical way to open up, but I believe this is the only way Patric can open up – completely and publicly. He has always been a man of extremes. I do know Patric well enough to know that if this works and he gets out of the mental hospital, we will see other books by him, roman-á-clef-type novels that will expose his innermost feelings about whatever he is doing or whatever relationship he may be in. I also know him well enough to know that it is in the safe play space of fiction where he will be able to expose his innermost feelings. In fiction, he can tell the truth while denying the facts to his friends, family, or lovers, who will no doubt be surprised to find themselves in his novels.

A warning, however, for those who expect Patric to have written anything that resembles a novel or to have written in any sort of standard novelistic style. He could not possibly do that in the state he is in, nor is it even his purpose to have written a novel. These are the writings of a madman, and that is how they should be taken. Sometimes Patric does explain himself through scenes, but there are other times where he just explains. The point of his writing this is to explain what happened – to himself as much as to anyone.

But I am getting ahead of myself. Patric is still in the mental hospital, even as I am compiling his works in some sort of order and writing this Foreword, and until he is out, I doubt he will be writing any novels. This account may be the only thing we can expect from him. Considering how things turned out, I would not be the least bit surprised if it were.

A few words regarding the details of how I compiled this book: after we discussed his writing it, whenever I visited Patric, he would give me whatever he had written during the week. He gave me pages and sections I preserved as chapters, so some chapters are short while others appear to start in the middle of a thought or scene. Patric sometimes wrote several sections before I could see him each weekend. The most difficult problems arose when he insisted I insert into the book (for we agreed early on that we should publish what he wrote as a book) fragments he had written before his hospitalization and had saved on a computer disk. He gave me verbal and handwritten descriptions of the pieces – prose and poetry – and I tried to find the pieces he told me about, but I cannot be one hundred percent certain what I included is the exact piece he wanted. I made notes throughout regarding anything I had to insert, to show where I was guessing. I haven't shown Patric the finished book – he said he trusted me and wasn't interested in details like the book's construction. He had written it and given me the instructions, and that was enough. I hope he's right.

But let me step aside. You haven't bought this book to hear me go on and on about my friend and these details that I'm sure interest you as little as they did Patric. No, you're here to read Patric's story – as only Patric can tell it. As for my involvement, I only transcribed what he wrote, without changing a thing, except the rare misspelling. I even left the exclamation points. These are Patric's words. I wouldn't think of imposing my own, of cleaning anything up in any way, of trying to put this into some sort of standard narrative, as one would expect from a novel written by someone in full command of their faculties. It is what it is, as Patric wrote it. The poems, too, are his, and were written in the mental hospital and suggested by Patric as the beginnings of each of the last four books. There was one poem he wrote that we couldn't find a place for, though I think it's appropriate for this book. It's a haiku titled "The Romantic,"

There's truly nothing
Sadder than a romantic
Without a lover.

I felt I should include it, since it so clearly states Patric's situation. But now it's time for me to step aside and let Patric speak for himself.

BOOK I

Chapter 1

When love becomes pain, only masochists remain in love. Which is what I am. A masochist. How else can I explain my actions? How else can I explain why I am here? What is there to say? I loved her. Sandi. I still love her. The question is, did she love me?

How can you know? Because they say they love you? Because of how they act? There's a song that says, "It's in his kiss, that's where it is," but how do you know if you haven't reached the point of kissing? Or if you don't get the chance? The truth is, you can only be certain of your own feelings, a painful restriction of reality. A pain I would gladly exchange for the whips of de Sade. A pain that taught me the truth of the first two wings of Amor. A pain that left Amor's last two wings lost to me – since Sandi would or could not return my love.

Where is my de Sade to flog me as I deserve? Bring on the whips! Draw the blood from my back, red rivers welling from stripes opened in my flesh. That pain can be no worse than this. That pain I deserve much more than this unendurable, unescapable, inseparable pain that refuses to subside and is now a part of me.

I don't want to be unfair to you. I should start at the beginning. This, I suppose, is a silly thing to say. Where else would one start? How else could I have you understand my mind, why I see in vain an amethystine comfort, a piece of mind I haven't felt for years?

You may wonder why someone found insane (or mentally ill, or some other term they have for my state of sitting, rocking, arms in front of my chest – thankfully punctuated by times when it's not too bad, when I can even manage to write – some sort of regression, I forget what it's called. Does it matter? It may matter to you, but you'll have to be satisfied with whatever I can say, whatever I can manage to remember or get past the barrier my brain set up, allowing only certain things through for you to see) would try to tell you his story.

First, you're not my psychiatrist. Second, I will not apologize for my madness. I have learned in my hospital stay to love it. I see Socrates was right – madness is superior to a sane mind. The sane mind is only human, but madness is divine. The Muses have inspired a frenzy, awakened lyric in this delicate and virgin soul. I have come in my madness to rescue those who are in need, who cannot see as I have learned to see. I seek and do not seek release from this calamity that afflicts me.

So why tell you my story? Why do I ask you to lend me your eye? My doctor and nurses say they care, but I know they don't. Not really. Not the way I need. In you I hope to find someone who can understand what happened in the only way that matters.

Chapter 2

Perhaps my mental illness frightens you? Don't fear. I'll try not to confuse. On most days my mind is clear. I hope my writing will be too. It's not my mind I can't control. Not really. It's my self, my body – my sufferings have met the blind eye of those I love – I've become invisible to those around me.

The story, my story. The story of the I. It's hard to decide when my story begins – everything is so connected. Should I begin with the first time I met Sandi, or with the meeting that mattered – the second time we met, the meeting that led me here? No. I should mention our first meeting, the story that preceded the time she caught my eye. That is important. I can't have you thinking she appeared out of nowhere. That would be confusing. Very confusing. And besides, even if she did not really catch my eye the first time, I am convinced I somehow caught hers.

I met Sandi my Senior year of college at the year's first Biology Club meeting. That was 1992. I'd been elected president the year before. I conducted the club's opening business, and we decided to work on several projects. I delegated authority, assigned heads of projects, giving a few to myself. When I asked who wanted to join what committees, Sandi chose every one I was on, volunteering for no others. I met her after the meeting, and we arranged to get together. We met once, but the projects fell through. I don't remember seeing her again that year.

No, wait. That's not the beginning. How can I say things began with Sandi? They didn't. They couldn't. How could they? No, things really began with me. Insanity's blossom may have been forced by Sandi's actions, but as with any forced flower, the truth is in the bulb, not in the tricks you play to get the tulip to bloom out of season. First, you have to know me – the me I once was. The me I have abandoned. You have to understand who I was to know the man I have become, the man writing you from this asylum.

I've been an adult my entire life. I preferred the company of adults as a youth – perhaps from infancy. I found adults more interesting, more stimulating, more pleasant to be with.

They made me more grown up, my mind strong. As a child, I would rarely even cry when I was hurt.

My mother told me of a time when I was two and playing with a glass jar. She told me not to carry it, but I did. I carried the jar around the house, out to the breezeway, and to the garage. Several minutes later, I came in from the garage, empty-handed. My mother saw me holding my arm against my side, and she made me lift my arm. My side was covered in blood. The jar was on the garage floor, shattered, one piece translucent red. Ashamed I had broken the jar when my mother told me not to carry it, I hadn't cried. But then, I never cried. Not when children picked on me. Not when I would get hurt, not when my parents would punish me.

I never cried when those I loved were hurt or died, whether it was my grandfather Molny, with whom I went for walks in the woods, and who had a heart attack when I was ten, or my dearest friend who drowned in a deep strip pit lake out at the Strip when we were both sixteen, drowned while I watched him from the shore, drowned while I swam to where he vanished, drowned as I dove into the deep waters, into the amethyst abyss to draw him up and out, limp and cold. Even then, as I drew my dear, dead friend out of the water, even when I went to his funeral, I did not cry. I was strong for everyone – at home, at the funeral home, at school. I listened to people's problems, everyone else's pains, tried to ease their pain by showing them how strong they could be, giving myself as an example – so strong because I never cried. I could take anything.

My early adulthood even spread to my clothes. In grade school I wore dress slacks. My parents did not make me – I wanted to wear them. I didn't wear jeans until my Sophomore year of high school, when I gave in to my friend, Niki, who had harassed me for years about it. I still didn't wear t-shirts, only button-downs in plains and stripes, keeping that style throughout high school, college, and the first semester of graduate school. I didn't know how to be casual. What kind of man can't be casual, cannot relax and enjoy life – cannot touch and caress and feel a lust for life that drives men to greatness and love and makes life possible? How could I have been this child? How could I have been this man? Everything was serious. Everything was politics. Existence was lifeless and cold. The walls against pain kept out the troops of joy as well. I enjoyed myself in the few ways I could: reading, drawing, walking. I did little else. This was life for me . . .

No! No! No! No! No! This was not life! I was a great despiser, an elitist without apology. I hated life and refused to live it. Perhaps I still do, though much of what I once despised are now the things I love – Pearl Jam, Nirvana, Stone Temple Pilots, T-shirt fashions, people's presence. I learned to love music as a source of Dionysian ecstasy, driving the soul, driving the world to greater heights. Yet people . . . the last in the list was a lie. I still hate people. I do have friends, the friend who, thankfully, is helping me out of my despair, but women . . .

My infancy was filled with women – especially the preteen neighbors across the street who helped my mother raise my brother and me while our father went to work in the foundry. My first friend was female, too – Cindy, born two days after me, and who I knew through babysitting. Also, my first cousin, with whom I was close, was a girl – my mother's brother's firstborn child, a few months older than I. Two constant companions, perpetual playmates, part of the beginning.

What does always associating with women and girls do to a man as he matures? I think, in the end, it must be harmful to his future female relationships. But I can only base this on my own experience, on my own case study – which is what psychology is based on anyway: innumerable individual case studies. While it's true that, as I grew up, I would befriend girls before boys, these early friendly, familiar relationships may have made later romantic thoughts of women more difficult. If you think of a certain sex as your friends, you have a hard time seeing them sexually later – a necessity if you wish to pursue more amorous relationships. The early animosity between girls and boys serves a vital purpose, and I missed the lessons it would have taught. Of course, my many male friends precludes, too, my seeing them as sexual. So I'm not gay. How ironic that my early friendships have only worked to make me unable to fall in love with anyone.

This doesn't answer whether I associated with girls early on because I felt more comfortable with them or if I was more comfortable because I was always around them. Nor does it answer why. Was it a natural predilection? Was it caused by being surrounded by women in my most formative years? Was it because most boys didn't want to be friends with me while I was growing up? Was it because two older boys molested me when I was young, forcing me into sodomy and sucking dicks in dark forests – something that should have made me either gay or homophobic according to most psychologists, but only seemed to make me more sexually repressed, despite an early, strong libido? Perhaps I avoided homosexuality and homophobia because one of the boys and I were almost caught one day in the woods, dropping clothes as we ran between the trees. I wasn't molested again by either boy after that. Until now, with my writing this, no one knew about what they did to me – my parents, my friends, even the doctors here.

Perhaps my sexual discomfort was due to some early semi-sexual activities with a young female friend while we were growing up – the sexual games we would play when she spent the night and slept in my bed – we were only eight and ten, and neither of our parents thought we would lock my door and explore each other and pretend we were a married couple in bed, sharing what we had learned about sex from those older than us, molesting us in the name of "sex education."

Now she dates men who call her and say she should "wear something easy to get out of" before they pick her up, while I can't talk to women, tell them how I feel, or even fall in love. Why the difference? Or is there a difference? Perhaps she cannot fall in love any more than I can. Whichever is true, I'm still convinced my casually comfortable relations with girls while growing up is what started me on the path to being uncomfortable with women later on, despite my strong and early sex drives, focused into sexual games and early masturbation – and especially the molestation – were the cause of my discomfort. Due to and not despite. It makes more sense to me.

My sexual feelings were further hindered by my being raised an independent Baptist, driving any interest in women further down, deep inside. Pastors and parents preaching the evils of sex, the church discouraging romantic involvement (this, at least, is what I felt) by not allowing boys and girls to sit beside each other in Sunday school or on the bus when we travelled, not letting us see these girls as potential dates or mates while saying we should only date and marry Christian girls. They insisted the eye offended – which left me nowhere to look. I know this contributed to my being unable to see women as objects of love and romance.

My church, as too many Christians everywhere, tried to deny the physical part of love and life – a part as important as the intellectual and emotional parts. All three are necessary for the fruits of true love to form. Intellectual attraction alone gives you friendship; emotional attraction alone is found between parents and children; physical attraction alone is lust. Philia, agape, eros – all three must be present, at least in part, to have true love. To deny one is to deny true love of that person – to deny one completely, as too many do the physical, is to deny true love at all. I realize this too late. I struggled against it even as I tried to integrate it with Sandi. Perhaps, if I could allow myself the luxury of such an integration, I could break through this unusual wall and be able to love a woman the way I want, the way I need. Perhaps . . .

Perhaps it's too late for me now. Could I find the kind of love I need while wistfully waiting for myself to return as I sit in sullen solitude? The answer, sad as it seems, is obvious.

I must admit, despite all of this, that I have met someone sweet while sitting in this asylum in impatient contemplation. I was sitting one day in the craft room, intent on my project. A staff, wrapped in grape and ivy leaves, topped with a massive pine cone – Dionysus' thyrsus – and, once I finished it, well, he and I took off to fly in intoxication and ecstasy across the room, lighting lightly before a wide-eyed girl, frightened and tempted by me. She wore an amethyst necklace, the small stone lying on her chest. I touched her lightly on the head with my thyrsus' cone, then bent and kissed her on the lips before the nurses took my arm and took my staff and led us both away. My projects have been more carefully monitored since then – a nurse has learned enough mythology to keep me from too much trouble and much less fun. I rarely see my sweetheart. I often wonder if she sees me.

But I should get back to my story, to the problems I've always had with women.

I've been on three dates my whole life. It could have been more, but I was afraid. It could have been more, but I wouldn't ask, fearing the physical, even the emotional – so I was left taking only two women out on three separate dates.

I somehow managed to take one girl out twice – once to the prom, once to a movie. That was it. There was no reason for me to stop. She was sweet. I liked her. She may have liked me – but we didn't go out again after our second date. In my fear of rejection, a fear I felt despite her agreeing to go out with me twice before, I didn't, I wouldn't, I couldn't ask her out again.

And these were not the only two women who caught my eye – or who were even attracted to me. I've had several women outright tell me they were attracted to me. But I wasn't interested. None were worthy. None were worthy, so I was alone, believing nothing was better than less than perfection. I looked for love with poor eyesight. So when perfection came, I was too afraid to ask her out, too inexperienced to know what to do. When perfection came, it left me in this asylum.

I should have spent more time dating, dating many women, hoping to find perfection – perfection to me, the only perfection important to a man. I was naïve in love, so I made myself vulnerable, unprepared for the love I've had to endure, and the pain it was bound to bring. How could I be prepared for love's vicious cruelties?

Chapter 3

I often wonder if I saw Sandi in that intervening year and a half. On much my memory fails. Especially on the things I find unimportant. People, especially. I have always had a hard time remembering a person's name – unless I went out of my way, which wasn't often. Few made such a sudden impression.

Sandi was the exception. The second time I met her. Perhaps I was less distracted. My academic interests were waning. I was burning out on biology. I was working on my Master's degree, but I began to wish it was in some other field. I was still interested in biology, but my interests were expanding. My passions for writing, philosophy, and economics were beginning to fill my focus. I'd even considered getting my Master's in economics. I didn't. I don't know why. At the time, I was more interested in economics, and I was friends with an economics professor who would have been happy to get me into the program.

I don't know why I didn't think of writing at the time, even though I was starting to write short stories, even a few poems. All bad. This book is the first writing I have done in a while – many months – and I would not have thought of writing again on my own. My friend, he brought me back to writing, to the warm comfort of words. No, I did not think of writing at the time, though perhaps, for many reasons, I should have. Instead, I stuck with biology – a subject I was already bored with, the teachers no longer teaching me anything new – which meant I re-met Sandi that spring, my second semester.

Sandi and I took two classes together, each auditing the one the other was taking, I microbiology, she evolution, hours back to back. She remembered me, name and all. I remembered her face, and faked it until the roll was called. Sandi Heideron. I didn't forget her name after that.

Chapter 4

The first day we re-met, after our two classes were over, Sandi asked me to have lunch with her. We walked across the campus to the closest Subway, smalltalking, getting reacquainted.

She reminded me how and when we had first met. She said she used to see me when she worked at the restaurant in my dorm, and that she had lost a lot of weight since then. Her face and memory became clear. She still had a hint of a tummy, a feature I found sexy, still find sexy in women, but no matter how much weight Sandi lost, she could never be thin.

Sandi was a naturally big person – some would say, big-boned. Not that I would have wanted her thin. Most men may have thought her too heavy, but I thought she was perfect. Women who lose too much weight have no shape. It feels like you're hugging a skeleton – or a twelve year old. I have no love for women who have to be skinny (I'm not talking about those concerned with being healthy, as Sandi was). Thin women are too vain and have no self-confidence. Who wants a vain woman with no self-confidence, who looks like a prepubescent girl?

That was one reason why I liked Sandi. She had no hang-ups about her body, other than keeping healthy. And her face – I love her face, smooth, oval, featureless, accentuated by a roman nose that made her more attractive. Eyes on the green side of gold, flecked in brilliant green. A splash of light freckles across her high cheekbones. Her hair was, well . . .

Once I was in the computer lab checking my email, and Sandi came in and sat next to me, planning to email a friend. In the middle of typing her message, she turned and asked, "Patric, what color's my hair?"

I stared at her hair. It was long, flowing across her shoulders in waves of loose curls, a natural mixture of blonde, strawberry blonde, and light browns. Then it hit me.

"It's calico," I said.

She smiled and turned to finish composing her message.

Such beautiful hair.

Sandi was an inch shorter than I am, and had a sexy body she kept well-hidden by dressing in baggy pants, loose t-shirts, over which lay an amethyst necklace that seemed out of place, but which her mother had given her, and open button-down flannels. In winter she also wore black combat boots and a heavy red jacket, but she always wore her baggy pants, loose t-shirts, and flannels no matter what the weather.

Chapter 5

We arrived at Subway. I ordered a turkey sandwich. She ordered a seafood sandwich. She said she was a vegetarian. Actually, a lacto-ovo-ichthyo-vegetarian. She would eat milk products, eggs, and seafood – non-terrestrial animals. Well, she wouldn't eat a whale or dolphin, either, although they aren't terrestrial. But they were. And I wouldn't eat them, either. Sandi frowned at my choice of animal. I decided then to avoid eating anything she wouldn't eat, at least in front of her – assuming there would be a next time. Why make people uncomfortable if you don't have to? Especially if you like the person?

We took our food to a booth and slid in opposite each other. We unwrapped our sandwiches, and Sandi started talking, asking what I had been doing lately.

"Not much. I've been trying to come up with a thesis project," I said. I took a bite of my sandwich and reached into the plastic bag and pulled the napkin out to wipe my mouth.

"Can't think of anything?" Sandi asked.

I had to swallow before I could say, "Not really. Everything I think of, we don't have the equipment to do it."

She shook her head.

"That's sad."

"Tell me about it," I said. "Makes me wonder what I'm doing here."

She cocked her head and gave me a quizzical look.

"Do we have the facilities to engineer a protein and produce it?" she asked. She took a bite of her sandwich.

"Yeah. You'd need the minimum facilities required by any molecular biology lab. Piece of cake."

Sandi wiped her mouth and said, "My riding team coach is an ag professor, and he's doing research with some kind of protein he's having a hard time getting enough of to do his research. He knew I was a biology major, so he asked me half seriously if I could make him some."

I shrugged, looked at her amethyst, her moving mouth, her green-gold eyes.

"Yeah. We can do that," I said. "If you find out the details from him, I could ask my advisor if he'd let me do the project. Maybe we can work on it together."

She sat up straight, smiled, and raised her eyebrows.

"Oh! That'd be great!" she said.

"So you're a member of the riding team?"

Sandi leaned forward, her eyes still wide. "I love horses. I ride in competitions all the time."

I smiled. An interesting coincidence. Niki, my best friend growing up, loved horses.

"Cool. How far have you gotten?" I asked.

"State. But I can't quite make it to nationals. Probably nerves." Sandi looked at her red tray. She squeezed her amethyst between her thumb and fingers, turning her finger mottled red-and-white. "Maybe in a year or two."

"Pressure's got to be tough at state level," I said. "Once you get beyond that, you'll be on your way."

I took a bite as Sandi looked up, her smile crinkling her eyes. Her fingers released her necklace.

"You're sweet. Of course, it could be that everyone at state is there because they're good." Sandi looked down again, and took a deep breath. "It would help if I didn't look ridiculous."

I arched an eyebrow.

"In some competitions, I have to wear this little Western outfit. Can you imagine me dressed in a fringe mini skirt, low-neck leather vest, and cowboy boots?"

I stifled a laugh.

"Exactly. Though I do have to admit that it does turn the eyes of the judges . . ."

". . . if they're men."

"Yeah. It's amazing how far low necks and high skirts will get you . . ." She laughed. "Though my boyfriend's not too hot on such tactics . . ."

I swallowed my food and disappointment. Great. A boyfriend. And I was really beginning to like her. She was the first person I had been this attracted to . . . ever. Oh well. I've always had one strong rule: don't try to break up a couple so you can have the girl. That rule hadn't been difficult to obey in the past, since I wouldn't even try to go out with single women – but it was one of my rules all the same. So it was simple: I wouldn't let myself fall in love with her. We would be friends. Period. Piece of cake. Still, I had to ask:

"Boyfriend?"

"Yeah. He's a math major, but he opened this store that sells used CD's, t-shirts, and beads. He used to work at the comic book store, but they screwed him and a couple of his friends, so they opened their own store. 'Jabberwocky's.'"

"Great poem. I've driven by the store, but I've never gone in. Sounds like an interesting guy," I said.

She looked out the window and sighed. "Yeah."

I raised my eyebrows again.

"He's a good guy. He's been better than any of my previous boyfriends."

"Really?" I leaned in, already breaking my rule in my heart.

"I've had a real string of winners. I dated this one guy who turned out to be married. It was my senior year of high school, and he was only a few years older than me. I met him at the movies. If you're married, don't you take your family out to the movies with you? Apparently, he didn't. We sat next to each other in the theater and talked until the movie started. We liked the same movies, and the same things, that sort of thing. And he was cute. When the movie was over, he stopped me and asked me for a date. I didn't think anything of it at the time, but the fact that all of our dates were at odd times and usually out of town and always ended at my place should have given me some sort of hint. Then, after a few months of dating him, I saw him in the mall, a young woman walking beside him. He was carrying a little girl, maybe two years old. I waved at him and ran across the mall and asked him who he was with. 'This is my wife," he says. Can you imagine? Good thing I didn't greet him with a kiss. Then he told her I was a student worker at his job. I don't think she bought it, though. When he called me again, I told him to take a hike."

I shook my head.

"What a jackass.'

"Well, guess what? He called me a month ago and told me he got a divorce and asked me if I would go out with him again. I don't know if he got a divorce or not, and, to be honest, I really don't care. I figure if he'd go out on his wife, he'd go out on me, too."

I nodded. We both had stopped eating while she told her stories.

"Good call," I said.

"The one before him was an alcoholic. He lasted a week. I only drink socially, so I wasn't about to put up with an alcoholic. And the one before him, well, we broke up after he received three paternity suits in one month. We'd been dating a year."

I laughed. "Sounds like you've had a string of good luck."

"Tell me about it. Before those, I had crushes, that sort of thing. In between, I dated off and on, but those were the only ones I considered actual boyfriends."

"I've only been out on a few dates myself. Prom, that sort of thing. Nothing serious. I haven't really found the right woman yet. I suppose it would be easier if I actually tried to date."

She stifled a laugh, rolled her eyes. "Probably," Sandi said.

"Hey, it takes some of us a while to learn the obvious," I said, and finished my sandwich.

"I'm the same way. Especially with my boyfriends."

Sandi stared out the window again.

I swallowed and leaned toward her.

"Is there something wrong? I asked.

"With me and Mick? Well, sometimes Mick can be difficult to get along with. Don't get me wrong, I do love him, but we've had problems."

I shrugged. "Well, yeah. All couples do. It's a matter of whether the person is worth the problem."

"Yeah. I guess so. We've been dating off and on for the past few months. I broke up with him once – when he hit me."

Chapter 6

Please excuse this break in my story. I had to stop writing for a day to cool down. I worked myself up too much, and I was lucky to calm down long enough to hide those past pages when I heard the nurses come. Or orderlies. I don't know what they were, those people in white; they were just interested in calming me down. Whether I wanted to be calm or not. After a few hours in restraints, I wanted to be calm.

Today I am in as much control as I was when Sandi told me Mick had hit her, even though there's nothing that pisses me off quicker than seeing a man hit a woman, and it made me mad to learn Sandi's boyfriend had hit her. I still seethe inside thinking about it. My release yesterday helped, so I think I can remain calm enough to write about what she said, about how she had pushed my most sensitive button.

If there is one thing I will not put up with, it is a man (if you can call such a thing a man) abusing a woman. I remember thinking that he should pray he didn't hit Sandi while I was friends with her. I was afraid of what I would do. I was likely to kill the worthless bastard.

I opened my bag of cheesy-feet.

Sandi fidgeted with her napkin, wadding it up and straightening it back out, over and over, as she talked.

"I told him to get out of my apartment and never come back. I wasn't about to put up with an abusive relationship. It's one thing to degrade me verbally, but it's another to hit me."

My hand went to my chest, smearing bright orange cheese in comet-trails across my black button-down shirt.

"Why would you put up with the verbal abuse?" I asked.

I definitely didn't like Mick.

"Because he's right. I am too fat, too messy, too insecure." (He was right about the last one, but I was never going to tell her that.) "He keeps me in my place, keeps me from thinking I'm too smart. I don't want people hating me because I act too smart."

I cringed as she continued:

"But I wasn't about to let him throw things or hit me. So I broke up with him and refused to speak to him for a week.

He cried and called me and stood outside my window and yelled for me to take him back until I couldn't ignore him anymore. I told him I'd go back if he promised not to hit me again. He knows if he does, I'll break up with him permanently, and nothing will make me come back. He promised, and he's kept his promise. He hasn't even gotten angry since then."

"Well, that's good. But still . . . I don't mean to get personal . . ."

"That's alright. I've been telling you my life story. I can't begrudge you your opinion." Sandi wadded up her napkin.

I offered Sandi a Cheeto. She refused. I took a deep breath and began. "Sandi, abusive people usually stay that way. He may seem like he's changed now, but I can tell you, he will hit you again. If a man hits a woman once, he'll do it again. It's a pattern such people rarely get out of."

"Well, he hasn't hit me since, and if he doesn't hit me again, I think I should give him a chance."

I looked down and noticed the orange smears and brushed the crumbs off my shirt with my clean hand.

"Okay," I said. "But what if you get married? What if he becomes abusive again once you're married? He'll know he has you, then. He doesn't have that reassurance now. You can leave him anytime you want."

Sandi shook her head and crossed her arms in front of her, bunching her breasts around her necklace.

"I can also divorce him anytime I want – especially if he hits me. And he knows I will, too."

"Divorces take time. And you'd be living with him, which I presume you aren't doing now. Those things make a big difference. And suppose you have a kid?"

"No, I'm not living with him – but, like I said, he hasn't done anything since, so I'm willing to give him the benefit of the doubt."

I raised my hands. "Okay. If you think he's changed, that's what matters. I don't know him. I thought, since you brought it up, I should say something." My fingertips were still orange. I cleaned them off with my napkin. Usually, I would have cleaned them off with my mouth.

"No problem. I appreciate it. And if Mick does hit me, I'd appreciate it if you'd remind me I said I'd leave him for good."

"Consider it done."

Sandi waved her hand, brushing off the entire conversation, then put her hands down on the table and straightened out her napkin. "Not that I suspect he will. He really has changed. And I love him very much. And he loves me. He's been very good to me." Her voice quivered as she said this.

"So why tell me this? You sound like you're trying to convince yourself you love him."

Sandi shook her head. "No, no, no, no, no. I really do. We're having . . . I don't know . . . it's hard to explain."

She hid behind her sandwich as she took a bite. Still, a green-gold eye looked at me over the curve of the crust.

"You sound like you're not very happy."

Sandi bobbed her head as she chewed.

"But I am," Sandi said, then swallowed.

"Okay. If you say so. If you're happy with him, then I'm happy for you. I hope you can work out whatever it is that's troubling you."

Sandi didn't notice I was speaking of her subtext, and answered as if she had actually said something was bothering her.

"Me, too. I don't know why I told you this. I didn't mean to dump this on you.. ."

I shrugged and raised my hands. "Don't worry about it. Any time you need an ear, I'm here. Look, I hope you're right. It's nice when you can find someone you care for and get along with."

Sandi nodded, then said, "Why? Haven't you found someone yet?

"No. Not really. I haven't found anyone I'm interested in. I'm not even going to consider a woman until I've confirmed she's met several criteria. If a woman doesn't share my values, why date her? She should also have similar interests. I mean, why be bored?"

"That's why I like going out with Mick. Our interests are so different, he stays interesting. I like learning new things about people. That's what keeps a relationship interesting."

26

Sandi finished her sandwich and washed it down with the last of her drink, which audibly exited up the straw.

"Well, yeah, there must be some amount of that," I said. "But you can't be so different you have nothing in common. Then they're no longer interesting, just irritating and infuriating, and it won't take long before you find you can't stand them. That's what's happened to me. No, you have to have the same values and hold similar beliefs. You have to want the same things out of life. Otherwise, there's nothing to gain out of the relationship. All you do is fight."

Sandi shook her head.

"I don't think Mick and I are all that different."

She wadded up her napkin and straightened it out.

"I know what you mean. You wouldn't want to date a clone of yourself – but the differences should only be apparent. Real differences, fundamental differences, those will always cause trouble in a relationship. And even people who appear to be similar can surprise you in ways that are a part of their personalities, but are not as surprising as, say, finding out your husband used to be a woman."

Sandi laughed. "Now, that would be too much."

"Yeah, but it's happened. Don't forget your previous boyfriend who was married. You don't want those kinds of irreconcilable shocks in a relationship."

"I couldn't agree more." Sandi wadded up her napkin and sandwich paper and stuffed them both into her plastic bag. "You ready to go?"

"Sure."

We stood and dumped our trays. As we walked out the door, I asked her, "Where do you live?"

"I live off campus."

"I live at the bottom of the hill. I guess I'll see you later," I said.

"See you later."

We parted at the door, but I continued to glance back at her until she disappeared. She glanced back once when I was looking at her. She smiled and waved. I smiled and waved back.

27

Chapter 7

The next time I saw Sandi was in class – the only place we saw each other, unless we planned otherwise. As we sat through the lectures, we conversed by writing in the margins of our class notes. Mostly it was smart-aleck comments about what was being said – things to make Sandi laugh. People would look at us as we laughed, wondering what was so funny. In Evolution, it was worse. The professor would make dry, understated witticisms and puns only Sandi and I seemed to catch, or at least laugh at. Everyone stared as we gave each other knowing looks.

One day, at the end of our second class, Sandi leaned across the aisle and asked, "Are you hungry?"

I said I was. It was close to noon, and I hadn't eaten. We both stood, grabbing our book bags.

"You have any place in mind? I asked.

"You up for Olive Garden?

I told her I was always up for pasta.

There's nothing more wonderful than Italian food. I eat too much of it. Or did. Or something. I didn't have to be asked twice to eat it. The sauce, the texture of the pasta. Pasta makes mere wheat flour delicious. And the different shapes make the pasta taste differently. Plain spaghetti does not taste the same as plain fettuccini.

And, Italian or not, I'm always up for a good meal with a friend. And I liked Sandi. She was turning into a good friend. We got along well. We had fun. She was a good friend. A good friend. Only a good friend. A lovely, beautiful, wonderful friend I wanted to be with all the time. She was dating someone else, so that was the only thing she could be or would be. A good friend. A good friend. Only a good friend . . .

"Can we take your car?" Sandi asked.

"Sure. If you don't mind walking down the hill to get it."

"Of course not," she said. She smiled at me as she grabbed my arm for a few seconds to follow me out of the building.

28

Chapter 8

Sandi and I left the biology building, chatting about microbiology and evolution. Applied and Environmental was everything I wanted in a microbiology class. I wasn't interested in bacteria that caused diseases. Way overdone. Bacteria that ate Styrofoam, produced hydrogen, or were magnetic – now that was interesting. My favorite bacteria were *Serratia marscecens*. They produce this pretty red dye, making bright red colonies – you have seen them on the ends of your lettuce, dying the stem red – though I'm sure the glow-in-the-dark bacteria on the fish would have been prettier had our lab succeeded in growing any.

We didn't talk about any of these bacteria. They were still future topics in our class. Come to think of it, I doubt we were talking about biology at all. Or maybe we were. I can't remember the details of every conversation we had – only the ones I consider significant. Even these I'm making up from memory, so the details may be off, though I think I've captured the spirit, and I know the topics are true to life. Maybe we talked about art as we walked down the hill that day. I know we talked about how we were both artist and liked drawing during one of our downhill walks, so I might as well say this is when it happened.

"So, you like to draw?" Sandi asked. "So do I. People tell me I'm pretty good, but I know I'm nowhere near professional."

I watched her walk beside me as we trudged down the steep hill, backpacks slung over left shoulders.

"I'm hardly a professional, either," I said. "My problem is, I can draw anything but people."

"They say people are the hardest to draw."

"No doubt. I guess we notice the subtle features in people that we don't notice in animals, since we see so many people all the time and so closely. Subtleties of nose and cheek and eye."

I looked at each of these features on Sandi's face. She noticed, looked down, and smiled. I smiled back and said, "Not to mention expressions. A generic dog or cat is much easier to draw than a generic human."

"Makes sense. There's really no such thing as a generic human. No such thing as a generic anything, really. We just notice human differences more. I'm pretty good at drawing people, but I have a hard time drawing anything else. Guess I'm backwards."

Sandi laughed. She leaned over to nudge my shoulder with hers. I laughed too.

"Everyone has their weak points. Sounds like we could draw one hell of a picture between the two of us, though," I said with a wink.

Sandi smiled. She reached out and squeezed my left arm, letting her hand relax there a second before letting go.

"It's a sad state of affairs when it takes two people to make a picture," she said.

I chuckled.

"Yeah. No kidding. I can just see us taking turns, you drawing the person, me drawing the background around him, the little dog on his lap."

"I guess that's why we're biologists," Sandi said.

We walked down the steep hill, pounding down the shadow-dappled sidewalk to my car, parked a mile from class in the shadow of the tallest building on campus, also the tallest building in Bowling Green, Pierce-Ford Tower, Dero Downing's last erection, the big brick dick.

Chapter 9

As I said before, at the time I was starting to get a little – well, more than a little – disillusioned with biology. This, despite the interesting biology on campus, the white squirrels around the Thompson Science Complex and the odd giant oval dandelions, each giant oval flower on a thick oval stem, encircled by a fountain of tiny flowers on thin, drooping stems, that grew around Pierce-Ford Tower.

The applied and environmental microbiology class was the first class I'd had in two years in which I'd learned something new on a daily basis rather than once a week at best or, more often, once a month. I read so much on my own, it wasn't uncommon for me to correct and update teachers in class.

Biochemistry II:

Professor: There's a good chance triple-stranded DNA is an artifact, since it can only be made in acidic conditions in vitro.

Me (after raising my hand): That's not true. I read an article this week that showed how triple-stranded DNA could be made in a pH of 7 with high magnesium content – which could be maintained in the cell with magnesium-binding proteins.

I couldn't do that in my micro class. Most of it was new. I loved it. But I still didn't like doing research. That troubled me, since research was the kind of life I looked forward to with my major.

There's not much you can do with a degree in biology except research. But I didn't like doing research. I liked learning about biology. I liked reading articles. I liked doing thought experiments and thinking about how to solve problems. If I encountered a problem in biology, I could usually figure out how to fix it or what to do. Just don't ask me to do the research to prove I was right. Let someone else do that.

I loved feeding my mind, knowing and learning new things, and using that knowledge to solve problems, to develop new ideas, to be creative. It was frustrating to know there was little market for someone like me. To be given the opportunity to use my mind, I would have to do the menial, manual labor that went along with it. It wasn't hard or difficult or strenuous – nothing in biology is – I just found thumb exercises a waste of time and energy. Time and energy I could be using to learn new things and solve problems others could test if they wanted – if that's what they liked.

Chapter 10

Sandi and I continued talking down the hill. Continued talking in the car. Continued talking in Olive Garden.

I learned more about how she and her boyfriend were getting along – heard her complaints against him – learned nothing positive. My heart saw the cracks in the wall, saw the barrier crumbling, saw its chance to find her love.

I began to fall in love. She needed saving. She needed to be saved from this relationship. He was still abusing her, but she couldn't see it. His abuse had become more subtle, more subtle than throwing things, more subtle than hitting her, more subtle by becoming psychological. More subtle because if the man is any good, the victim doesn't know she's being abused. And he was good. She did not have the eyes to see what he was doing to her.

So I fell in love. She needed saving. I was in love, but I couldn't tell her I was in love. It would only drive her from me, and if I drove her from me, I couldn't save her. I wouldn't tell her I loved her. I could help her and hope she would fall in love with me. I thought she was already beginning to. She wanted to spend too much time with me.

She would deny it for a long time – deny it until denial couldn't mask her feelings from herself and her eyes were opened so she could see everything I had done for her. Then she would find herself in love with me. Psyche would finally fall in love with Eros.

BOOK II

I love you enough
To want you for myself
So I can know for sure
That you are safe
And loved

Chapter 1

Sandi first let me know how she felt about me when she asked one day if I could take her to equestrian practice. Of course I could. A measure of friendship is what you will do for your friends. And Sandi was my friend. Besides, I had an opportunity to spend some time with her.

As I drove down the tree-lined road, we smalltalked about what she did with the equestrian team, about what she wore at competitions – she was still embarrassed she had to wear her Western cowgirl hats and outfits. They were the opposite of her personality – it was hard to imagine her dressed in a leather skirt, boots, vest, and cowgirl hat with her sitting next to me in her flannel thrown over a t-shirt and jeans. By this time I had started wearing t-shirts too, mimicking her style of dress.

It was embarrassing, now that I think about it. I didn't have the right clothes to be mimicking her style. I wore my plain button-down shirts over some t-shirts I happened to have but rarely wore. I was sort of yuppie-grunge. But that night we laughed instead at the absurdity of her competition costumes.

Then, as we neared Western's farm, fence-lines replacing tree-lines, Sandi's mood turned serious. She looked at me until she caught my eye.

"Uh, please don't take this wrong, but I don't want you to stay while I practice."

"Sure, no problem," I said. "How come?"

"I don't like people I care about watching me practice. Even my dad hasn't been to any of my practices," Sandi said.

"Okay," I said. "No problem."

Then it hit me. I was someone she cared about. A Freudian slip, or a simple reference to our friendship? It seemed strong words for a friend. Pressed, yes, I would say I care for my friends. Pressed further, I'd say I loved my friends. But I wouldn't volunteer to say I cared about someone if I were talking about them as a mere friend. Who would? Every word has both connotation and denotation, and the connotation of saying you care for someone is understood by everyone to mean you care for them in more amorous ways than mere friendship allows. Since this is true for everyone else, why wouldn't it be true for her, too?

Sandi fingered the amethyst necklace on her chest.

"I'll find someone to take me home, so you won't have to come back to get me," Sandi said. "But I don't want you to just drop me off, either. I want to show you around, introduce you to everyone. But when we start to practice, I want you to leave, okay?"

"Whatever you want," I said.

She smiled.

"Thanks," she said, then pointed. "Oh, the farm's right up here."

I saw the sign for the farm at a turn in the fencerow and clicked on my turn signal as I let up off the gas.

Chapter 2

We pulled into the farm's gravel lot. I parked and we got out. Sandi showed me around. I was introduced to everyone, horses and humans alike. The horses were beautiful – as though a healthy horse could be anything else – long noses, strong bodies, deep chocolate eyes.

Sandi handed me an apple. My mouth caressed the apple's skin, smooth, supple, luscious, before I took a bite, then handed the rest to a wide-blazed horse, who did not bother with such small bites, engulfing the dark red fruit in two, lips caressing my palm. I wiped my saliva-wet palm on my pants when the horse finished the apple, then followed Sandi around the farm.

Sandi brought me into the arena as the sky turned dark. She showed me around the indoor arena, her practice delayed by a tractor tilling the ground, providing soft riding dirt. Sandi pointed out everyone, who she liked, who she didn't like, and why. Then finally, too soon, they were ready to ride.

Fulfilling her wishes, I left – willing and unwilling – for the love I felt for her. To make her happy, I would leave. I wouldn't want her to be uncomfortable with someone she cared about watching her practice.

Someone she cared about.

I think I took her to practice a few more times. I never saw her ride. I remember seeing some women riding once, but Sandi wasn't supposed to ride that evening. The trip was for some other reason, long forgotten.

Sandi loved her horses as much as Niki did. They both loved to ride. It was Niki's parents' hope that the two of us would grow into more than friends, that our friendship would grow (along with my size, as she was, and still is, taller than I) to love.

It didn't happen. We couldn't see each other as anything more than friends. It was my hope that Sandi would see us as more, as I already did. There was never anything remotely sexual between Niki and me, but the tension between Sandi and me worsened every moment we were together.

Chapter 3

Since Sandi's riding required a cowgirl hat for certain routines, I took her and her cowgirl hat to the mall one day, entering a Western store, a store no one would expect to see either of us in, so she could get her cowgirl hat – I still laugh at that – reshaped. While we waited for them to steam and shape her dark tan hat, she said, "You've never seen me wearing a cowboy hat, okay?"

I smiled.

"I haven't, yet," I said.

"Well, you're getting ready to, and if anyone asks, you never saw me wearing one."

I looked at her with mock-innocent eyes.

"And if they don't ask?"

"Please don't tell anyone," Sandi said. "I don't want anyone to think of me this way. My boyfriend hasn't even seen me in a cowboy hat."

"Well, don't I feel special?" I said.

"Don't. It's nothing special to see me in a cowboy hat. I don't like anyone seeing me in the stupid thing."

I understood how she felt – I would have felt the same way, indeed, felt ridiculous just being in the store. Yet here she was, involving me in a part of her life she hid from everyone outside the riding team. I was being brought closer to every part of her life, to parts of her life she hid from her boyfriend. Why would she allow me to be so close? To be, in this case, closer than the man she said she loved?

When they finished reshaping the hat, Sandi tried it on.

She looked as cute as one can look in a cowgirl hat – though I was beginning to think that no matter when or how I saw her, she looked cute. It's amazing how the more you fall in love, the more attractive a woman becomes, transformed before your mind. Love makes you see depths of beauty previously unperceived. I wish I could see her face, so clear in my mind, to see the beauty I once saw in her. Then it fades, in seconds. And now I see so little that is clear, only the post-impressionist strokes I have painted. Distance, and maybe madness too, have clouded my mind from her – clouded

40

her in many ways, but intensifying her in others, driven
sharper, clearer into my mind.

Chapter 4

How many nights have I lain awake? Sleep escapes me. I have no one to hold. I only want to hold her – to hold a warm, soft, loving body next to mine, her warmth, her breathing, her presence able to put me to sleep. Lullabies made with the simple touch. Where is my Pera to offer her breasts? I languish, dying of thirst – a thirst for love, a thirst as desperate as any for water. I die of thirst in this prison, but no Pera comes for me. I died as Cimon surely would have, had his daughter failed to quench his thirst.

Presence is all I need. Her fingers on my back, along my spine. A touch. I grip my pillow, trying to, trying to . . . But it's not enough. Not tonight. All attempts in vain. I need a loving presence. Tonight is worse than most. Why can't I have love? Love. Hate. I'd hate love if I didn't need it so much. Where is love? Where did it go? I haven't seen it. I don't know. I need, I need . . . Touch, feeling, feelings, love, hate, pain – anything other than this terrible emptiness. Hollow. I feel like throwing up. I'm nauseated. Can love, a lack of love, make you sick? I'm not in that kind of hospital. I know what kind of sickness it can cause. But physical illness? I still need love. I'm still in love. Love. Need. We need love. Why can't I have a touch? Someone to hold close? To call mine? Tears run down my cheeks. I must have a touch. A loving touch. Someone to hold me before I go mad. Before I cannot, dare not, know not love forever. Ahhhh! I run my fingers through my hair. I touch my back. Nothing helps. Only the presence of another. The presence of another I cannot have tonight no matter how much I need it. Shall I sleep tonight? I don't know. I must try. I must try. I must try, and so good night. Maybe I can get the emptiness to vanish in the night. Maybe I can lose myself in dreams. Maybe I can go to sleep. Maybe.

I often dream of Baubo's dance,
Bare midriff sensually tantalizing,
Bringing Demeter
Smiles of her love for life,
Transcendent high above her sorrows
For the loss of Persephone.
I dream she can bring me
Out of the darkness
With her movements,
With her life,
As Ame-no-uzume
Did for Amaterasu,
Bringing life back to an unlit world
From the depths of her hideaway cave.
I also dream of Bes and Beset —
Each abandoned me to the evils
They were meant to protect me from in life.
Such sensual protectors
Apparently preoccupied one with the other
When I most clearly needed them both
Close by my side.

Chapter 5

I often visited Sandi at work. She worked in an office on campus and was often free to talk. I talked to her there on the days when our classes did not meet. It was in her office where I first met her boyfriend. I have to admit, I liked the man – he was interesting in an intellectual way. But he said very little, so I honestly can't say much about him, though he kept a wary eye on me until I left. I remember seeing him only twice more. Both times, Sandi and I had gone to his store for a few minutes to tell him we were going out to eat together.

On Valentine's Day, we didn't have class together, so I went to see Sandi in her office. My mother made me Valentine's Day sugar cookies – frosting-decorated hearts and bears – and I took some to Sandi as a Valentine's Day present. What else would I do? She smiled, and appreciated the cookies her friend had brought her. For lack of a chair, I sat down on one knee, talking, when a professor we knew walked in.

The professor gasped, took a step back, and said, "Oh my! Oh, I'm sorry to interrupt! You two are obviously deeply involved in something here I have no business interrupting."

Sandi and I looked at ourselves and each other, realized how things looked, with me down on one knee, and burst out laughing.

I stood.

Sandi put down the cookie she was eating and said, "No! No! Come on in! What do you need?"

"Are you sure? It looked very serious. I wouldn't want to interrupt a romantic moment or anything."

"No romantic moment. We're just talking," I said.

"Well, if you're sure . . ."

"We're sure," Sandi said. "What do you need?"

But how sure were we? Nature had dictated the position we were in and, as Jung once said, nature never lies. The professor had only interpreted what she saw. She was probably more accurate than either of us. We were, after all, only the scene's authors.

Chapter 6

What do I remember of our relationship? My memory muddles with time. Some days are difficult. Today I can think of nothing, only my feelings. Last night was difficult. Last night has given me a day of difficulties. I'm hyper. I need to do something.

I have so much nervous energy, I don't know what to do with it. I can't do anything about it here. Hardly. My mind is darting, darting with my nervous hands. Some days I feel like Erzulie Ge-Rouge – I feel like huddling in a corner with my knees drawn up, fists clenched, tears rolling down my cheeks. But I know they won't look too kindly on my doing that – they'd think I've gotten worse.

I have. I've gotten worse in many ways, better in many others. I never needed to be touched like this before. I don't understand this mania. How can I? This could be solved so easily, but no one will do it for me. I can't even do it. I am the only one who can. No one else can. But how can I? I don't understand. I never have.

Why can't I do it? Why can't I love? Why can't I be in love? Why do I deserve this? I just want love. That's all I wanted. Why can't I have that? Erzulie Ge-Rouge may weep over the shortness of life and the limitations of love, but she cannot understand as well as I the pain of such knowledge. How can she? She cannot see with human eyes. She is merely a goddess. She is immortal. It is we mortals who have to live with this knowledge.

How can we? To know immortal love is an illusion of our short lives, to suspect that love itself may be a biochemical illusion. I would love if I could, but I won't be allowed. You cannot love without a lover. So long as I live without someone to love, I cannot know love. It's only a transient illusion.

45

Chapter 7

Have I found love again? There is a girl, a woman, who lives here. I've learned all about her. A tragedy of fear and innocence. She, too, wanted to love and to be loved and to live a happy life in love. Her love, like mine, simply can and will not be.

Rocking gently, she sits
Touched, now untouched since.
Her tears long dried,
Her soul since died,
She talks no more to no one.
Children heal,
But not all wounds.
The deepest wounds remain unhealed,
A permanent shock
Shattering sheltering shores
She kept protected.
Shattering the tiny soul
Before it bloomed.
Shattering her entire life
Before she learned to live.

I cannot help but fall in love with a soul this sorely damaged. That's what put me here, this concern for damaged souls. I see I'm doing it again – I'm doing for her what I did for Sandi, doing again what I've done to myself, knowing and doing it all the same – but I cannot abandon her, this girl who needs love more than I.

Chapter 8

There may not be much left to say about my relationship with Sandi. A relationship that sent me to this locked-door life, and this is all there is? We saw each other every other day in class, and tried to fill the other days with lunches as an excuse to see each other. That is mostly it: classes and lunches, times to talk, though sometimes our excursions changed. Whether it was these odd excursions or the many unchanging times we spent together, similarity wearing us down, I don't know. But I will relate what I remember and hope it explains – if not everything, at least enough.

I remember one day after class Sandi asked me if I would do her a favor.

"Sure. What do you need?" I asked.

"I need to buy a mouse."

"You need to buy a mouse?"

I don't recall ever needing to buy a mouse.

"For my snake," she said.

That piqued my interest.

"You have a snake?" I asked.

"It's a milk snake. It's really pretty. If you take me to the pet store, when we get back I'll show it to you."

We sounded so seven. Still, I was happy to hear her say such things. I love unusual pets – especially snakes – and I hadn't been to her place before.

"Sure. One mouse, coming right up," I said.

We talked our way down the hill, as we did every time we went out to eat, often Olive Garden, our restaurant of choice, where I had begun trying many vegetarian items. Then we were on our way to get a mouse for her snake.

After we bought the mouse, she invited me up to her apartment. There, she introduced me to her pets, starting with her beautiful red, orange, and yellow milk snake, which made a quick meal of the little mouse we bought. She also had a rabbit and a tank full of fish. Like me, she preferred unusual pets.

I visited her apartment only a few times. I don't remember what the other reasons were. Once I think I may have brought her some books – though the ease of letting her borrow the books in class makes me suspect my memory there. We used our two classes for much more important things than learning biology – like learning more about each other. There was a time when we were writing notes back and forth in class, as we usually did, and for some reason, she asked me what I was looking for in a girlfriend. In response, I wrote the following in the margin of my notebook:

A tender heart,
A love-filled soul,
Libertarian,
Loves rock-n-roll.
Loves to touch,
Loves holding hands –
When I'm upset,
Will understand.
A scientific mind,
Artistic core
With lots of spirit
To make us soar.
A love of life
And natural things –
Loves to read
'Bout everything.
Will love and care
For me all my life –
The woman above's
My perfect wife.

After she read it, Sandi wrote: I know plenty of women like that. I'm their queen.

I wrote back: I'm glad to hear that.

After she read it, I realized what we had written, so after class I tried to clear things up.

"I hope you didn't misunderstand what I wrote during class. I . . ."

"No, I didn't misunderstand. Don't worry about it."

I didn't think anything else about it.

That's a lie – to both you and myself. I still wonder what she meant. Most people would interpret it as her being interested in me. That's what I thought. Who wouldn't? What else could she have meant? Was she interested? A logical interpretation. But then, I often wonder what logic had to do with our relationship. It certainly wasn't rational. No amount of reason could rescue me from this dilemma, and she refused to use reason. So what could I do? Reason is only helpful when dealing with rational people. With irrational people, who knows what will happen?

Chapter 9

In the same way I thought I knew how to interpret her note, I thought I knew how to interpret what happened several days later. I was sitting in my dorm room, probably reading, probably watching television, probably writing. The phone rang. It was Sandi.

"Are you going to be studying tonight?" she asked.

"I don't have any tests coming up, so probably not."

"Oh. Well, I was wondering if you would like to study together tonight, but if you have nothing to do, I guess . . ."

"No, I, uh, I probably ought to be studying something. You want to meet somewhere?"

"If you have a study room in your dorm, I'd like to come over there."

"Yeah, there's a study room here. But my roommate's gone, so I don't think we'll need it."

"Okay. I'll be right over, then."

I didn't know what to expect. It was the strangest conversation. It was an excuse to come over. I knew that. It was so transparent, apparent. I could only wait for her arrival.

A knock on the door. I was in a co-ed dorm, so she didn't have to check in at the desk. She came up. She knocked. I let her in. We talked.

I forget what we talked about, but I do remember it led to my telling her the entire story of *Les Miserables* up to the point I'd read. I told her how wonderful the book was, a wonderful story. I told her about the chapter, Chapter IV of Book Fifth of Fantine, the third paragraph that begins, "Let us say, by the way, to be blind and to be loved, is in fact, in this earth where nothing is complete, one of the most strangely exquisite forms of happiness."

What a proposition! Hugo then follows this with such a beautiful proof that we must agree that this idea is one of the world's simplest truths. It was this I read to Sandi. One of the most beautiful passages of prose put to paper by mortal man. This paragraph shocked and stunned me so much I became a Hugo fan for life. And so I am. And so I will ever be.

It was perhaps exposure to such ideas of love that led me to this state you see me in. How can you read such beauty as, "The supreme happiness of life is the conviction that we are loved; loved for ourselves – say rather, loved in spite of ourselves, this conviction the blind have. In their calamity, to be served is to be caressed. Are they deprived of anything? No. Light is not lost where love enters," and not be affected?

But what of a life without love? No amount of vision can cut through the darkness surrounding such a soul. The desperation of a loveless life blinds the clearest eyes, makes beauty pallor. How can beauty live in a loveless soul?

This is what I read to Sandi, hoping she could see the beauty I saw, and in so doing, bring her closer to me in spirit, and then, perhaps, in love. Our talk became closer, more passionate, until . . . It always happens. Something would have happened between us had my roommate not returned with about ten of his friends. Nothing kills the seeds of passion like interruption. Passionus interruptus. We had to abandon my room for the study room, bringing our books with us, books we had ignored for the first few hours she was there.

In the study room, we talked about biology. A young man overheard us and asked us to help him with his homework. Further interrupted, we were unable to return to any semblance of personal conversation. Finally, Sandi said she had to leave. I offered to drive her back to her apartment, but she refused.

I should have insisted. I should have asked her why she really came. She didn't want to study. We may have studied fifteen minutes. It was an excuse. Each of us knew it. Cowardice prevented anything from coming of it.

I'll never be sure why she really came over. Maybe she was beginning to fall in love with me, too. The tension between us was tangible. Maybe there was some fear there as well. She was still with her boyfriend. Maybe she felt guilty, too. After she left, I stood at the window and watched as she walked up the hill, returning to my room once she vanished under the lowest branches of the trees that lined the sidewalk.

Chapter 10

Our conversations crossed currents of thought carried candidly. Wonderfully walking, whispering, waking while we tentatively talked tantalizingly to do through who knew what we'd do. Speaking of past boyfriends, of a past boyfriend she found was married, of a past boyfriend who had children near her age, of her past problems and possible preventions postulated for her current boyfriend and possible future ones. Her complaints about her current boyfriend continued without ceasing, increasing in momentum, in length, in time.

Considering her complaints, one wonders why she would want to stay with such a man. His abuse had become more psychological without the physical outlet. She couldn't see it. She said she was lucky to have him with all her faults – from looks to personality. I couldn't find the faults she described. They were ones he attributed to her and she now believed.

The biggest fault I could see was with her self-esteem. Why didn't she think better of herself? Obviously he wouldn't compliment her the way she needed. Quite the contrary, from her reports. Would I have to do that for her? Could I do it for her without it appearing to be what, to be honest, it was meant to be? It would be difficult, but I would try for my love.

BOOK III

I rush out of the house
Awakening in time to miss breakfast.
Cool air hits.
It's nearly Fall.
Only a few days left of summer.
I run down the drive,
Bordered by dying flowers –
Where was I when they were beautiful?
I reach the blacktop.
A lone car pulls away.
I've missed her
As I've missed so many in the past.
Perhaps I can catch her
If I run
And make myself known
Before she's out of sight.

Chapter 1

What love nourished my soul, tore me through, blinded me and made my eyes see clearer. I hadn't felt more focused in my life. I wanted to succeed for her. I wanted to achieve for her. I wanted to live for her. She was what I would live for.

It was the life I wanted so much for myself. A life in love – I was in love with being in love as much as I was in love with Sandi herself. An intertwining of souls. This is what I felt was happening.

Perhaps I was more aware than Sandi – she was in denial, grasping in desperation to the love she used to know with her boyfriend. A love she didn't know, but denied the knowledge, the lack of knowledge. Why was her desperate grasp for someone who treated her better than she expected, but worse than she deserved? Why did she need to punish herself? Why did she desire de Sade's whips? She felt she deserved no better than the excuse for a relationship he provided, so she must have felt she needed punishment.

How many conversations did we have where she said she deserved no better than the way he treated her, and wondered why she deserved being treated so well? The overhead threat of violence and the constant psychological abuse – these were how she was treated well? How would she act, how could she act, if I could persuade her to love me? I couldn't be the punishment she wanted in a relationship. I couldn't see that then, so my heart still pursued her.

Chapter 2

In this state Sandi and I left together for Lexington to look up articles at the University of Kentucky for our project. I think then is when it really hit her that I was falling in love with her. She perhaps began to think so when, as part of the planned trip, rather than my taking the rational route of following her to Lexington, then driving back to Bowling Green while she drove her car home to her mother's to get it fixed, I suggested following her to her mother's so she and I could travel to Lexington together. It was hundreds of miles out of the way, but she agreed. She was beginning to understand. And so was I. Why else would she have agreed to such a plan? Hers made more sense. But she agreed to mine instead. The implied suggestion was clear.

I followed her. She took me to her mother's job so I could meet her mother. A wonderful, sweet woman. She noted Sandi was wearing the necklace she had given her. The visit was short. We had a way to go. Hours more on the road. Her car dropped off, we left together, heading east to Lexington.

"Do you want to talk or listen to music?" she asked.

"I don't care. I brought my tapes if you want to look through them. Or we can talk."

"I have a headache. Let's listen to some music."

She chose Stone Temple Pilots. *Core.* The player started playing "Sex Type Thing." It was not a sex type thing. We sang along. Somehow during our singing, she made a comment about not being as pretty as Sinead O'Connor. I said she was. She flustered and became embarrassed, thanking me. To ease the tension, I said O'Connor would be prettier with hair. Sandi said, "I was talking about my singing."

Oh.

We made the rest of the trip in silence, the heavy rain heralding in the night.

The trip back was better. We spoke sporadically, though mostly about our research. While we were at U.K., she said she was thinking about something she wanted to do. I asked her what it was. She was reluctant, but I pressured her. She said her now-wet toes made her want her boyfriend to suck on them. I wished she hadn't said it. Afterwards, our discussions stuck to business.

We went to her mother's house. Her mother fed us and showed us her unusual pets, including a large African toad. The food was steamed broccoli and a vegetarian pizza. The pizza was horrible, but I didn't want to say anything. When her mother left the room, Sandi saved me from silence by saying she thought the pizza was terrible. I didn't want to insult her mother's cooking, but with such an opening, I couldn't disagree. We disposed of the pizza. After a short visit, I left for Bowling Green. Alone. It was late. It was dark. It was raining. It was a three-hour drive.

Chapter 3

A turning point in our relationship – perhaps a warning, perhaps . . . Who knows what it could be interpreted as? On a day, I vaguely, no, don't remember exactly when – though I know it was late into the relationship and well after I had fallen in love, Sandi and I left together after class and went somewhere. I curse my vagueshadowed memory somewhence. It can e'er be unfair to you. But we left and returned to the building we'd left, talking along the way. Perhaps we had gone to get a campus paper, for I know we were each reading one when we got to the biology club room to sit. But no matter. We sat and read in silence, when suddenly Sandi looked up at me and said, "Do you mind if I'm blunt?"

"No," I said.

Sandi rubbed the amethyst of her necklace a second, looking down at it. She looked up at me.

"Are you hitting on me?"

I had no idea what to say. I wanted to tell her how I really felt. Then carefully, purposefully, I told her the literal truth and lied: "No. Why do you ask?"

I hadn't been hitting on her, but I was in love with her.

"My boyfriend wanted me to ask you. It's very unlike him. He's usually not jealous."

I put down the paper I was reading.

"Why would he think I was hitting on you? Why would he be jealous?" I asked.

I tried to catch her eye, but she scanned the paper she was reading and would not look up.

"I'm sure it's because we hang around all the time, and go out to lunch more often than he and I do," she said.

I nodded.

"He shouldn't worry," I said, "because I don't break up couples. I think it's cruel. And it rarely makes for a good relationship between the new pair."

"Well, I'm sure he'll be glad to hear that."

When I told my friends what had happened, what I'd said, they couldn't believe I hadn't taken the opportunity to tell her how I felt.

I wonder what would have happened had I told her the truth.

But I didn't tell her the truth. There is no point in second-guessing yourself. The past is just that. We mustn't dwell on it, but learn from it. Et cetera, et cetera.

I say this and yet, I am living here in this asylum. I cannot let go of my past. Sometimes it's easier to know the truth than to live it. If I would take my own advice, I'd have far fewer problems. I wish Sandi had chosen to hand me her garlic-blossom sooner. It would have caused us less pain. But she didn't. She wouldn't have meant it.

Chapter 4

Though the next few weeks were uneventful, Sandi continued to affect me more and more. I was falling in love and had no outlet. This creates the ironic result of depression. Maybe it's not so ironic. If something builds and cannot leave, it gains in weight. Besides, what's so joyful about being unable to have the one you love?

I couldn't take it any longer. I wrote her a letter. Maybe I'm a coward, but I couldn't make myself come out and tell her what I felt.

I knew my tongue would get in the way of the words I wanted to say. Why my tongue cannot emulate the abilities of my fingers is beyond me. But I wrote her the letter and left it with the secretary at the office where Sandi worked, someplace she could get it without my having to mail it to an address I did not even have.

It was a terrible letter. Such a terrible letter. I bared my soul and waited for the results. I received it in a phone call. She asked me what she should do about what I said. Should she write me a letter or should we talk about it right then? I am proud to say I refused to let it go. We talked. Our conversation was a good example of why I wrote the letter. The letter may have been good, but the number of times I stumbled over my tongue was embarrassing. But it had to come out into the open. I only wish it has been more effective.

Chapter 5

Naturally, this isn't the actual text. Sandi has the only copy of the original. But Patric said he did his best to recreate the letter he wrote her. He does think, though, that it was probably twice as long as the one he had provided for us here.

Dear Sandi,

I can't think of how to start this letter, but I feel I should write it no matter the consequences. My continued silence is too wrenching. I can take it no longer. I love you so much. I love you and I cannot put off any longer telling you I love you.

I know telling you I love you will ruin our relationship. I know it will, and I know you won't break up with your boyfriend, no matter how much you need to – not for my sake, but your own.

The days I spent with you have thrilled my heart – even when you told me everything your boyfriend has done to you. Actually, that's not true. Every story you told about how he treats you made me angrier. It bothers me that you would consider staying with him after what he has done to you.

Do I have to remind you of the stories you told me about him, of the time he threw things at you? Of the time he hit you? You say he stopped the abuse after you broke up and went back to him. He hasn't. He still abuses you. Only now, it's psychological.

He makes you feel worthless, like you don't deserve someone as good as him. But you deserve better. You're a beautiful, wonderful person who deserves nothing short of pure happiness. You don't deserve the abuse you get from him, abuse that will only worsen over time. Abusive people don't change. They wait until you're trapped, and then the abuse returns. If you marry him, the physical abuse will start again.

You deserve better. You deserve love and happiness, the kind I can give you, my ideal. But you are everything I want in a woman – not perfection, but perfect for me. You remember the list I made? You said you knew plenty of women like that, and that you were their queen. You recognize the truth. There's no one more perfect, no one I enjoy being around and talking with than you. We talk for hours when we get together. Remember when you came over to study, and instead we talked? We have the same loves, the same passions. Who would be happier together than we would be?

Nothing could make me happier than being with you, and no one would make you happier and feel more loved than I would. Your boyfriend doesn't love you. He's obsesses with you. He wants to possess you. I want to love you. Abuse isn't love. Obsession isn't love. What I feel, what I'll give to you, is real love. It's the kind of love that will make a man change, as I have tried to change in so many ways, to change the things I know you dislike. It's why I've become a vegetarian. I did it for you.

There's one thing I hope never changes, no matter the consequences of this letter, and that is our friendship. It's silly to hope our friendship can survive such a revelation should you reject my love, as no friendships have, but I hope this one does. I would hate to think such a good friendship should be ruined over this. I know it will, but I had to tell you, before your not knowing made me more depressed. Hearing you say either way, whether you love me or not, is better than the torture I've had not knowing. And losing your friendship because of this would in many ways be worse, though I know I will lose it. But I finally had to let you know how I felt. I had to say I love you. Because I do. I'll deal with the consequences as they come.

Love,
Patric

Chapter 6

I sighed as I dropped my pen. My flurry of writing ended as suddenly as it had begun. I felt drained. I looked at the handwritten pages for a minute, then opened the desk drawer. I rummaged for an envelope, found one, folded the letter, sealed it in the envelope, and turned off the desk light. I sat in the dark for a few minutes, then forlornly pushed the chair back and moved two steps to the bed. Television. I stood, turned it on, collapsed on the bed. A video by Alice in Chains, "No Excuses," came on. Perfect.

Chapter 7

Drunken language hurts the same as the pain it tries to kill. It doesn't kill, only heightens, heightens hurt and pain. I wonder what the purpose of this will bring me, will it bring me gain? I doubt it will. Drunken stagger brings me closer still to the pain I wish to now avoid. But who else can I blame? I don't know what I should do, to fall this drunken way. Should I stay sober in my pain? This drink only makes it stay. Why won't it go away?

Chapter 8

"Could you make sure Sandi gets this?"

I handed the envelope to the woman behind the desk. She knew me. I had come to see Sandi often enough.

"Sure. No problem," she said.

"Thanks."

I left quickly, hoping Sandi wouldn't come in. I was fortunate. I walked to the classroom.

"Hi, Patric," Sandi said, smiling.

I smiled back. My face and actions did not betray me – she could see nothing amiss.

"Sandi! It's been so long!" I said.

"Yeah, at least fourteen hours since we had dinner together. Where have you been keeping yourself?"

She raised the corners of her mouth along with her eyebrows, widening her eyes.

"Oh, here and there. Say, what're you doing Friday night?" I asked.

I sat in my seat on the front row, center. I dropped my backpack onto the floor beside me.

"Well, my boyfriend and I were going to go hiking and have a picnic. Why?" Sandi asked.

"What about Saturday night?"

"Nothing."

Sandi looked at me, her eyes soft and showing curiosity.

"Would you be interested in seeing a play? Anton Chekov's 'The Sea Gull' is playing on campus," I said.

Sandi sat up straight and smiled.

"Sure! That'd be great," she said.

"Great. I'll get the tickets," I said.

I bent over to unzip my backpack and pull out my books.

"How much are they?" Sandi asked.

I put my book and notebook on my desk and said, "Oh, a few bucks. Don't worry about it. I'll get it."

"No. How much, exactly? I'll give you the money now." She dug in her pocket for some money.

"No, no. My treat," I said. "I'll pick you up at 6:30, and if you still feel bad about my paying, you can buy me a mocha at the café afterwards."

"Deal. Oh, better yet, one of my friends is going to be making us crab fettuccini alfredo. I wanted you to come anyway. We can go there, then go to the play afterwards."

"Sounds good," I said. Italian.

Sandi looked away and said, "Hi, Dr. Jenks."

The professor entered the room. He smiled at Sandi and me.

"Hello, Miss Heideron, Mr. Molny, class. You ready to learn about bacteriology today?"

"Sure. Why not?" Sandi said.

Dr. Jenks smirked.

"You better be. There'll be a test soon, and I plan to put everything I know on it," he said.

"Gonna be a short test, huh?" I said.

The room laughed, including Dr. Jenks.

"Why don't I set myself up next time? You two are bad enough when I don't," Dr. Jenks said.

Smiling, we gave a simultaneous, "Thanks!"

Dr. Jenks rolled his eyes. He turned to the blackboard, still shaking his head, and started his lecture on *Lactobacillus*.

Chapter 9

After class, which was held in Thompson North, Sandi and I walked toward Thompson Central together, where Sandi worked, talking. Her apartment was in the opposite direction, but I thought nothing of it. We often talked while walking from class before she turned to go home. As we paused in front of Central, Sandi looked up and said, "Oh, could you wait here for a moment? I need to go in and check something."

I watched her walk into the glass-front office, and felt my stomach drop as I looked in horror. The secretary handed her the envelope. Thankfully, I had written nothing on it – she could recognize my handwriting. I released my breath when she shoved the envelope into her backpack without looking at its contents. Had she looked, I would have bolted. Or maybe stared, immobilized by horror. Or thrown up. She exited the building, we exchanged a few words, then parted. I was relieved, but now it was too late. It was finished.

Chapter 10

That night and the next day I paced my room, shaking, wondering how she would respond, fearing I knew. At 7:38 the next night, the phone rang.

I answered.

"Hello?"

"I . . . I don't know what to say."

Sandi's voice quivered.

"Sandi, I . . ."

Words evaporated. My shaking worsened. I needed water.

"Do you want me to respond with another letter, or do you want to talk about it? Sandi asked.

I closed my eyes, breathed deep, kept my eyes closed.

"Well, since you're on the phone, we might as well talk about it. I . . . I wrote the, uh, letter because I write much better than I c . . . can talk. Especially about something like this. But you're here, so let's talk."

Okay. I read your letter, and . . ."

"And?"

I squeezed my free right hand into a fist.

"And I don't know . . . I . . . I'm not going to break up with my boyfriend. I really do love him . . ."

I don't believe that. I don't believe that. I don't believe that. I can't believe that.

"But after all he's done to you . . ."

I sat on my desk chair.

"He's really not that bad . . ."

I stood. I could not sit.

"Listen, in all . . . of our conversations . . . you never said anything . . . anything good about him. Never. And every time you said you loved him, it was as though you were desperately trying to force it past your lips. Why? Why is that?"

I stepped to my bed and sat on it, perched on the edge.

"Well, we were kinda having problems . . . and I thought you might like me, so I didn't want to . . ."

"Say anything good about your boyfriend? I'm sorry, but I don't understand. Most people would try to discourage someone by telling them how much they loved their boyfriend, not by bad-mouthing and complaining about him . . ."

I lay back on the bed and stared at the fluorescent light over the head. It was tinted red, the light.

"I don't know . . . All I know is I love him, and I . . . The feeling's not the same with you, for you, I mean . . ."

I closed my eyes. Lights flashed behind my lids.

"Listen, Sandi, I love you. I love you very much. Your relationship isn't right. You deserve better. You're a better person than that. You don't deserve what you . . ."

"Patric, I'm not all that. I know what you said in your letter, but I'm not perfect. I'm not everything you make me out to be."

A deep breath. You are. You are perfect. MY perfect. Perfect for me. I grabbed my pillow, laid it on my forehead for the coolness.

"I didn't say you were perfect," I said. "I know you. I love you, not because you are perfect, but because you are who you are. I love you, perfections, imperfections, for each of them because they are a part of you. I love you. You're perfect for me, you're better than I could expect. You say you're not all that, but you're everything I want. Isn't that sufficient? I . . . It's just that, you're everything I wanted. Everything, and . . ."

"Look, I'm sorry, but I . . . I can't. I love my boyfriend. I'm lucky I have him. Sometimes I wonder why I deserve someone so good . . ."

The pillow grew warm on my forehead. I shoved it off.

"Sandi, you deserve better. Why run yourself down? I think you're wonderful . . . You deserve so much better. You don't realize . . ."

Tears rolled down from the corners of my eyes, wetting the tops of my ears.

"I'm sorry," Sandi said. Her voice quivered. "I can't. I . . . I really do love him. And I don't . . . I don't . . . Look . . ."

I sniffed, tried to muffle it and my own quivering voice.

"I'm sorry I brought it up. No matter what my feelings for you were doing to me, I shouldn't have done this. It's probably ruined our friendship and . . ."

Sandi's voice lost its quivers.

"I don't want that, Patric. We can still be friends. Can't we act like . . ."

"Can we? Act like it never happened?"

My left ear ached, I held the phone so hard against it. Sore and wet.

"I . . . hope . . . Look, I don't think we should go to the play Saturday . . ." Sandi said.

"I understand," I said. "I'll go by myself."

"I'm sorry, Patric." Sandi's voice broke.

"Goodbye, Sandi . . ."

"Goodbye. I'll see you next week, I guess."

My stomach squeezed, pushing into my throat.

"In class," I said.

"In class. I'll see you in class. Bye."

She hung up. I dropped the phone on the receiver when the dial tone told me she wouldn't return. I looked back in longing to see if she was there, and lost her forever. I wandered to the window and stared through the dirty glass. Trees and hills spread in lush greens, darkened by the night sky, highlighted by the full moon. I pulled the shade and wandered to my bed, lying on it. My roommate arrived with several friends, turning on the lights as they came in. I stood and left and went for a long, quiet walk. Tomorrow would be Saturday. I would go see the play. I went in a melancholy mood. I was moved by how close the mood of the play approximated my own.

BOOK 4

Darkness, shadows fall about
Permeating all throughout.
Within our souls, within our minds –
Look within, see what it finds.

Looking close, a point of bright,
Wondrous, glowing, shining light.
Small and tiny, growing slow,
It comes for all the world to show.

Where has it gone, what has it been?
It once was here, now gone again.
A bright and glowing priceless treasure –
Can it now be gone forever?

Chapter 1

With wonderful wicked warrior wails, a potent, powerful priestess asked, "What's love got to do with it?" One wonders what life would be worth living without it, when a radio god, famous for his belligerent bellows, lets slip a wisp of worrisome wisdom: love is the only emotion you cannot control. It is not a second-hand emotion – it is vital to life. So I sit, lacking love – it's why I no longer truly live. It's why I now merely exist.

Man cannot merely exist. Not for long. No. He must have attributes. He must live. I exist – an exasperated existence, existence desiring exit, in this hospital I call home. Existence is mere survival, as plants and animals survive. Less. I am relegated to less – my existence is dependent on others' benevolence.

So I sit with others, waiting, waiting for the Corybant to come. Perhaps they will come and dance for us today, as we so desperately need. I sit and wait, desperate, for a visit from Eros, a visit from myself.

Eros has been cruel. I don't know why. Maybe Eros will catch me a new love, a woman to finally for the first time fall in love with me, to love me as I need. Perhaps the lovely lass within these walls will finally fall in love with me.

I remain unloved for Eros' negligence to strike a woman with love for me – though he has struck me hard enough, struck me mad with love, from love, without love. Ah, Juliet, my sun, my morning star, where are you? Why won't you love me? Why is your lack of love such pain? The pain of unloved lovers pulses through, pulses. A golden arrow pierced my heart – hers was gold mixed with lead. I was driven mad with love – while she preferred her punishment. And now I feel my heart is dead. My heart, it pumps no more.

Chapter 2

I was alone. I am alone. I'm alone and I don't know why.

I don't know why I lie when I know the truth. For reasons I cannot ascertain, I can't seem to say what I want to whomever I wish to love.

It's hard to love or be in love when you can't say what's on your mind. But then, how can your difficulties but increase when the woman you love turns you down?

Okay, so she did have a boyfriend – but I find it hard to understand why she would prefer a loveless relationship to the one I had to offer.

Maybe women find me too kind – maybe I don't know what women want. If they want abuse, they'll be disappointed with me. Which is why I think I'm now alone.

Maybe it's because I treat women as subjects, not objects, and they really want a man who acts as though they're objects. Have I predicated my love life on a feminist falsehood?

Perhaps it's my depth of soul. People say they hate shallow people, yet it seems only the shallowest can find someone to love, while those with great depth of soul and learning seem destined to be forever lonely.

No one really hates shallow people – the shallow's happiness proves the opposite. The man of depth, depth of spirit, depth of soul, depth of knowledge, depth of wisdom, depth of love – it takes so long for such a man to achieve happiness, if he can achieve it at all.

Throughout history, most men of depth have lived their lives in unhappiness. That's the story of Faust. Does their greater understanding of the world cause this? Does knowledge breed cynicism, and great knowledge breed great cynicism? Is it the nature of the knowledge? Is it false knowledge – or misinterpretation of the facts – that causes unhappiness in great men?

Or are ignorance and shallowness really bliss? The goal of philosophy is twofold: greater understanding and happiness. What irony if the two are incompatible!

But what if the ignorant and shallow are really not happy, but living lives of quiet desperation, as Thoreau said? It seems the only choice is a combination of wisdom and optimism, a combination difficult to achieve, as the history of mankind has shown. Perhaps the man of great depth will only find such happiness when he has finally learned to love with a passion worthy of his depth, and finds a woman worthy of his love.

Chapter 3

Sandi and I talked little after my letter. That summer, she disappeared, accepted by a special marine science program in New England – Massachusetts, if I recall. Since I went to summer school, Sandi kept in contact through e-mail. They read like nothing happened, then stopped the day she went to sea.

We saw each other once that Fall, and found right away there was nothing we could hide. So it came as no surprise I didn't see her again for another half a year. When we did see each other again, we tried to act as we had before, but there was a tension there we couldn't ignore.

It was weeks of thankful separation before I heard from her again. It would be the last. The semester was almost over, November was barely in the air – winters sometimes go unfelt in Kentucky until February. I returned to my apartment to find a note on my desk. I held her number in my hand. She'd called a mutual friend to get my number and left a message with my roommate for me to call her. She must have called sometime Thursday, since I had been gone all day, only coming in Friday morning. I tried to call her Friday. She wasn't home. Nothing but the answering machine. I had to wait. What could she want? It may be nothing. It could be everything.

Chapter 4

The phone rang near noon Saturday. It was her! Yes. What do you want? What do you need? She came right to the point. Could we see each other? She had some books I had lent her and she wanted to return them before she moved to Louisville. Oh. Why are you moving to Louisville? Her answer was vague. School was mentioned. Tension tore tremors through the telephone. I wanted, needed, desired, was dying to see her. But what could I say? What should I say? I was certain she was still with her boyfriend. She still had school left. Why was she running away? Why would she leave? Why would she want to finish school in Louisville when her boyfriend still lived in Bowling Green? I said she could keep the books if she liked. She thanked me without disagreement and hung up. I haven't heard anything from her since – not a word in voice or e-mail, language lost between us, cutting us off forever.

Chapter 5

I write this sitting beneath the oak tree in the hospital's yard, and I wonder what the squirrel whispers to the sky. Does he tell her of my mind? Does he tell the gods what I now think of them? How else could they know to drive me mad with misery as punishment? What else could explain the squirrel's ceaseless scurrying up and down the tree except as medium between the gods and me? No one believes me, but I know it's true. They say it's another symptom of my madness, but I know what the squirrels really do. They chatter too much to chatter about nothing.

I mentioned I was living in an apartment when Sandi called the last time. In May I had moved into an apartment on Kentucky Street with a friend. It was only a few blocks from Western's campus and their abundant white squirrels that are slowly spreading through Bowling Green from the campus. Once I got my roommate a job, the arrangement was ideal. First shift, I was in class, he slept. Second shift, he worked, I did whatever – read, wrote, did homework, watched T.V., played on the Internet. I was writing a book. A terrible book I burned shortly after finishing it, while I was living with my parents. Third shift, I slept while he played on the Internet (well, the MUD mostly). We saw each other for an hour between his coming home and my going to bed. It was almost like living alone.

This time alone afforded me time to write. Mostly poems and short stories, though sometimes my misery would break through and I would have to write whatever was on my mind, what I tried to cover by writing external rather than internal fiction, for fear of exposing my soul. I feared showing my soul, a fear that finally drove me mad. But I did delay it with my writing. I don't know if this delay, this way of dealing with things, really helped or hurt. Should I step aside and let you read it, to perhaps decide for yourself whether it was a therapeutic delay, or a way to drive me mad sooner?

Patrick sent me a note with this section explaining the paper he's talking about here, and I hope I've found the right one among the papers he left me to take care of for him. I may be wrong, but this one seems to make the most sense in the context of what he wrote. If I am right about this paper, I must remark that at least Patric's memory still seems sharp. Maybe when Patric gets better, he can tell me if I was right, and future editions can be corrected, if necessary.

Why am I so fucking miserable? Why the hell have I painted myself into this fucking corner, into a field I have grown to hate? Why can't I write like I want to write? Why didn't I go ahead and get a Master's in English? It would have made me a hell of a lot happier. Instead, I have to do some stupid biology experiment I don't give a damn about to get a degree I don't want.

I keep doing what others expect of me instead of doing what I want, what will make me happy. When May comes, that will be the last I will see of this damn college, or of Bowling Green.

I need to get some stories published, to make myself a writer. The one story I've published is far from enough. If the screenplays Jimmy and I are working on don't do something, I don't know what I'll do.

I'm so tired of biology. If I never took another class, if I could avoid biology forever, it would make me ecstatic. At least it would be a start. I need a stabilizing factor in my life. I need to be in love.

What is so difficult about that? What is fucking wrong with me that I can't get anyone? Why won't anyone fall in love with me? I can't get any fucking interest. I must be too nice a person, too good, since all the fucking assholes seem to have all the women they want, and more. Apparently, if you only want to fuck women and toss them aside, you can get all the women you want. If you treat women like fucking whores, like pieces of meat, they'll line up.

What the hell is wrong? There are people like me, who would love them, cherish their love forever, treat them like queens, adoring them. But I am alone, and men who only want sex are not. Why?

Why have I done this to myself? I should have gotten my fucking Master's Degree in English, focusing on writing. That's all I want to do. It's what I care for. It's the one thing I have consistently stuck with. Why do I have to go with temporary safety instead of taking the chances that would make me happy?

Maybe that's what I should start doing. In May, I'm out of here, either way. Whether I've graduated or not, I'm leaving. I can't stand it any longer. It's time I took my own advice. I'm good at giving advice, but terrible at listening to myself.

It's time I started living for myself and not for others. I know what's what will make me happy, and yet I am here, getting this Master's Degree in Biology to please my parents. They think their money's wasted if I don't pursue this path. That's not true. I'm tired of living under this veil of guilt. Whose fucking life is it, anyway? They're not the ones living it. I am. I appreciate all they've done, but why should I be obliged to them in such a way that it makes the rest of my life miserable?

There are few joys in my life, and these obligations I've given myself prevent me from pursuing them. In the truest sense of the word, I have been sacrificing, and it has done nothing but make me miserable. That will happen no more. I will finish this semester, and then be through with it. Then I will dedicate my time to doing what I love.

I have found the truest joy in my writing. It's the only time I'm happy. When writing a short story, working on my novel, or working on one of the two screenplays I've started with Jimmy, I am happy and at peace. When I'm doing biology, I can't wait for it to end.

What kind of life lies ahead when you dread what you are going to do? That's the problem. Doing biology. I hate doing biology. What I love is thinking and talking about biology. I'm a theoretician, a thinker.

That's what I love about writing. I don't consider it work. Writing is the means by which I best express myself. That's why I love it. That's why I want to write more than anything. That's why I will continue to be miserable until I can dedicate all my time to writing.

Why can't I do what I love? Why did it take me so long to realize that what I wanted to do, the only thing I really wanted to do my entire life, is write? Through everything I wanted to do or be, I have been writing. I was writing in grade school, when I was interested in sharks. I was writing in high school, when I was interested in plants. I was writing in college when I was majoring in Recombinant Gene Technology. I am writing now, as I'm working on a Master's in biology. Why could I see, why couldn't I acknowledge that what I really wanted to do was write? Why can't I now? One would think that, after the compliments I have received my entire academic life from different teachers on my writing, I would have gotten the hint. And now, within the last year, I finally figured out what I should have known all along: I am a writer.

I have heard that to be a great writer, you have to suffer. I don't know how true that is, but I do know I am suffering over my decisions. If that's true, I should be doing some of my best writing now. Maybe I am. Maybe I'm not. I don't know. I'm really not sure how helpful this is or has been. Maybe it is. Maybe it isn't. I don't know. It hasn't solved my problems. It hasn't given me someone to love. And it hasn't given me what I need to give up everything and become a writer.

But maybe it has relieved some mental pressure. Still, a little writing, a small rant, won't change a thing, won't really help me at all. What I need is a change, a change in myself, a change in my life. I need to quit lying to myself and to others about how I feel, about what I want. It's time to face things as they are, not as they should be – to make everyone face the decisions I have reached, and to live with them myself. If I don't, I will continue to be miserable.

Chapter 6

This, which he sent me a few days later, seems to confirm my suspicions that I chose the right paper. It also confirms my assertion that his memory is still sharp.

I stayed miserable. I wasn't going to change. I thought I had come to a realization, but I hadn't. Not where it matters. I had not achieved the self-knowledge necessary for my surface realizations to become reality. I hadn't reached a true epiphany.

The truth is, I maintained my academic path because it was expected of me. It's hard to change your river's flow. I wanted my friends' and parents' acceptance and respect. I didn't want to disappoint people. And in trying to gain these things, I lost respect for myself. I was more alone then than I had ever been.

Chapter 7

I loved living alone on Kentucky Street. I had time to myself, time to think and read and write. Time to grow lonely, even among my friends, until I began to fear living alone. Now, I fear living alone. I need to be loved, I need someone there for me, someone to live for me as I live for them. Two, one, alone together, together alone. A part of each other, nothing apart.

How can I love a loveless life? I cannot stand what I seem to want. I want to be alone, but not alone. I want to be alone with one who will live her life in love with me.

Why? Why? Why? Why can't I have that? I want to be in love. Such high standards make love hard to find – but not impossible. An irony. I have become withdrawn, and now I run the risk of remaining without love. Withdrawn more and more, fighting to survive, setting up defenses to protect myself. Do I stand a chance? Can I stand, make a stand against the creeping abyss, threatening me with its stare? Madness. Madness. Madness!

Chapter 8

It has been days since I have written. I've been distracted.

First, my girlfriend is gone. No one will answer my questions. Where is she? Where has she gone? No one will tell me. No one will let me know. Perhaps they fear what I will do?

Second, I was lucky to have hidden my papers from the nurses. Now they are safely smuggled out of here. They can't know what I'm doing. If they learn, they could make things worse.

They think my writing makes me worse. Worse or better, it needs to get out, it must be written. I want the world to know and see – they must understand. They must! The nurses also don't understand my need for music. My music moves, motivates, mellows my madness. Specifically, they won't allow me to hear Alice in Chains' "No Excuses." They say it makes me worse. But the only way I'll know I'm over her is if I can hear the song without it pressing my mind into the abyss.

Ever since our conversation over the letter, when I turned on the television to MTV, and the video to "No Excuses" came on, I have found the song intolerable to my mental health. I will not turn it when it's on – I insist on hearing it, but it always sends me into serious depression. Still, I need the song. They do not understand that an Apollonian depression is preferable to a Dionysian madness, or even an Aresian anger!

I believe I was telling you about my year in my apartment. I abandoned the research project Sandi and I had planned to do, and I conceived another, a project I soon became bored with, having become bored with biology long before. I wrote a lot – poems and short stories – every one a failure. I failed at starting a libertarian literary magazine. I failed to progress on my thesis project. I failed to get any positive responses to my hundreds of resumes I'd sent out. I finished my classes that Spring and moved back to my parents' home. While there, I wrote a rant, a bit clichéd and really not much of a rant, to be honest. But it was honest. I thought I had come to an understanding, but in truth, I was sorely lacking in epiphanies.

Again, I hope I am correct in choosing this from among his writings. The instructions he again sent me seem to suggest he is talking about this paper. I must admit, it is difficult to put together a solid work from among these fragments he sends me or sends me instructions to find.

Sometimes you take the wrong road, and you think it's right. Whether it is a college major or a career choice, or a choice between reading philosophy and reading fiction, the wrong road can make you miserable.

So it's time to get on the right road, to scan down it, to learn that on a hot day there are mirages that distract you and send you off doing things that, in the long run, don't even interest you. My life has been resplendent with examples of my mistaking the road I'm on, thinking I want to take the road, only to find it's not what I want. I know what road I should be on, but I avoid it, taking the detours away from what I love.

I'm educated in science, molecular biology, and I have taught myself a range of things that would make a life beautiful – that would drive you mad with passion at knowing, learning, loving what you've found. Astrophysics, quantum physics, the beautiful nuances of chaos, philosophy.

There's nothing more beautiful than Nietzsche – his writing inspires, whether you agree with him or not. The power, his words, the wonder, making you want to achieve the greatness he envisions for everyone, if only they would realize their own potential. The greatness of man recognized by Nietzsche, whose love of life is addictive, who makes you want to make a world as he thinks it should be, as it could be if only we would realize we're capable of greatness.

But philosophy, even the most beautifully written, still cannot meet the greatness and beauty of fiction, a poetical prose, full of meaning, the love of the word leaping from the page, making you stare in wonder at the very page itself, wondering how simple black and white can create such color, such beauty, such magnificence, to drag us from our dreary lives into an exciting world of the imagination.

Why do I want to write? How can I help it? To have the power to create your own world, to bring people alone on a journey you have created – how can you not want to live such a life?

What does it take to be a writer? Pen and paper will not suffice – a typewriter or computer will not do. They are but the tools. It is imagination and experiences you need.

I have the imagination. I have the computer. I have the pen and paper. But where are the experiences? Six years of college, four as sheltered as my high school years, certainly did not give me the experiences I need.

My life began two years ago, with a love lost – a love never gained – and the pain and new life it brought back to doldrums, realizing I shouldn't be in biology, realizing I should be writing instead.

With such a realization, how can you find the impetus to go on with your thesis project, especially where I am now and where I need to be to work on it. An hour drive can make a difference when you have a job, or are looking for one.

Jobs have been hard to come by around here, and so has inspiration. It has been months since I have done anything creative, especially since I started writing my weekly column for the opinion page of our newspaper. It is less creative, but it is writing, and it deals with several of my passions: politics, economics, philosophy, government, society. I can talk about art, about books, about the things I love, so long as it stays nonfiction. But fiction, the creative, mythical worlds of my own creation, this is what I love the most, this is my truest passion. It is what I must get back to doing. I must get back to my love.

My literary experiences are many and growing. I have finished *Still Life With Woodpecker* by Tom Robbins and am starting Jack Kerouac's *On the Road*. I have read and loved the great master of fiction, Victor Hugo, from the *Hunchback of Notre Dame* to *Les Miserables* to *Ninety-Three*. I cannot understand how anyone could go through life without reading Hugo. Then there is Dostoevski and his darker view of life, whose writing is a gem in the crown of literature.

What am I doing? I've gone through six years of college for something I no longer love. I have sent out hundreds of resumes from coast to coast to find a job in this unloved field and received nothing. What does it take to get a job? I entered molecular biology believing it was the way to get a job, as writing would not open up many horizons.

So here I am, making money, albeit a small amount, writing articles, while I wait for someone to call me for a job interview in biology. But if they do not realize my talents soon, I must move on, for I cannot, should not, and will not sit still now or any longer. I must look, investigate, find what I am looking for. I had hoped to do it with someone, with a love, but I must move on alone – for now.

I must live in a dream to think I can make it as a writer, to achieve greatness doing what I love. I will settle for simple survival as a writer, but it is survival AS A WRITER that I desire. A writer of what, maybe it doesn't matter, but writing is the life, the love I want to, will to, will achieve so I can be happy, truly happy, perpetually happy for the first time in a long time since I began to wonder why, what, wherefore for my life, for my choices. Where am I and where am I going and will I make it alive – who will make the journey with me, or will she be there when I arrive?

I know I can't achieve true happiness without being in love, but my prospects there have been less than forthcoming. I was once in love, and I am certain that, at least to some degree, she may have been in love with me. But when the time of truth came, she chose what she had over what could have been.

Maybe it was a mistake to fall in love with someone who had someone, but who can control falling in love? There is little chance I'll fall in love with someone around here, which I suppose means there is as little chance of my soon falling in love at all. It is another reason why I need to get the hell out of here. This place does as little for the experience of love as it does for the experiences needed to write.

I guess that's what I get for living in a small town my entire life. It's not my fault, of course, but I can and should do something about it now. I guess I'm still too cautious to do something as insane as taking off, though there have been times I wished I had enough money to do so. That has always been my excuse: the lack of money. And I'm more than willing to admit that's exactly what it is: an excuse.

Excuses overrun my life, making me, driving me
Cautiously against a part that forever wishes to drive,
Drive, drive alone, down the road, away from it all,
Away from everything I hate, I love, I dream,
Toward an unknown future, toward a rising sun
Exploding in brightness, exploding all my fears, all my excuses
Making me wish, dream, want, desire the unknown, the unseen,
Until finally, before I know what has happened, I am stricken
By my cowardice, driven down, down, down,
Deep into a despair I cannot know or understand,
Until I am forced to rise, forced to triumph in spite of myself,
Forced to triumph, to recognize
A greatness I may have never known.
I wonder sometimes where I'm going,
what America has in store –
If America has anything in store for me, and if it ever will,
Until I realize she has nothing for me
I don't create for myself –
Excuses must go before I can succeed, and succeed I must,
Succeed I will, despite myself, despite everything, despite all
No matter where I go, run, hide, in spite of everyone,
Where, helped or not, I must do it, no excuses,
Excuses gone, forever, to force my cowardice to the surface
To be smitten, struck down in hatred before
it gets all-consuming,
Before it destroys me as it has so many others,
As the burning desert sun has destroyed all in its path
And creates mirages on the road and
in the sand and in our minds
Before we realize what has happened to us and our lives.

I've been told you you're not suppose to write poems like this, but I could care less what others think of my art, so long as I'm happy with it. I wrote it as it came to me, as I am writing this, as I will continue to write this. Is it stream of consciousness? Almost. It's maybe too structured for that – I don't know. Themes and points, purposes have arisen in paragraphs that seemed to have formed of their own free will. There was a purpose in them, in all my ramblings throughout.

Chapter 9

I rambled and ranted in my writing, lying to myself. I had moved back home. My parents' home. A mistake. I realize now it was a mistake. Within a week of moving back in with my parents, my best friend, Dillon, got me a job working with him as a security guard.

This job as a security guard may seem superfluous, but to understand why I sit in sadness in this asylum, you must understand how I felt about this job, how it only worsened the damage to my psyche. It may be as much at fault as Sandi was. She only forced the bulb to bloom out of season, setting the course for my insanity, making it come when it did.

My entire life I was in control. I never failed at anything. I was far more intelligent than most. I saw so much below me.

I love sitting my days under the oak in the yard, shade protecting me from summer sun that burns but gives her life through the dark green leaves. I sit and feel calmer, satisfied. But I wonder if I should feel satisfied here. If I feel satisfied here, is this tree really my companion in salvation, or is it instead my zaqqum-tree? Perhaps I read too much in a day's simple pleasures. I lay back and fall asleep in my oak-tree shade.

Security guards – my best friend excluded, of course, as he was intelligent, only unmotivated – were far, far below me. Yet I reasoned I could use the time positively. Since I only had to sit in a shack at night for eight hours, I reasoned I could get a lot of reading and writing done. I was right.

I read constantly. Economics, fiction, philosophy. Von Hayek, Dostoevski, Nietzsche. Months of incessant input, no matter the content, drives men mad to speak, to share, to be heard. Incessant imbibing of information intoxicates and drives men mad when there lies before them no possible intellectual output. A man can only absorb so much before there must be some sort of personal output – he must share his new knowledge with someone, mull over new ideas. Writing is not enough. You must hear your own voice. You can't just write – you have to tell. There was no one in all of Marks County with whom I could talk.

Not true, there were two, but due to the hours I worked I couldn't talk to one, and the other, Dillon, had work to do, since he was a Captain. A Captain. Oh, captain, my captain. Captain of the guard. Gallantly protecting an earthen scar, a patch of shale shoveled around. Mon Capitan. Mon ami. Driven mad by guarding mines.

I'd begun to feel unworthy of myself, of my expectations. The only employment I could find was as a security guard, despite my education and intelligence. Soon it became apparent – not at the time, but all too clear now – that my reasoning that my time working at the mines could be used for writing, and that my writing would keep me sane, was wrong. I did have time to write. Plenty of time. But my writing turned out not to be enough. I needed intellectual stimulation from more than books, an outlet from more than writing. Solitude was insufficient to keep me clear of mind – I couldn't survive a hermit's life. I thought I preferred solitude, but now I found it intolerable.

Boredom set in despite my books. Despite the C.B., I had no one to talk to. I felt the end of conversation drawing near, killing me as it will kill the last remnants of humanity and sanity left in the human race. What will happen to our minds when we can no longer talk? Will we be wards of those who can still converse?

So I sat in little huts – a chair, an air conditioner, a shelf, a clock, a C.B., and sometimes a radio, especially if I brought one. I sat in my box, six by eight, a window, a door, a dark night of solitude, the only light coming from my shack and the overhead lamplight set on an electrical pole. The only thing I had to do was read and write, read and write, read and read and read. I wasn't kept at one shack for long. I was kept moving through the summer, through the months of May and June, until I was occasionally put in charge of the tower.

I loved the tower. Especially during storms. I would listen as heaven's laughter rolled across the sky and watch as the glint in its eye sparked the buoyant cloudy haze, obscuring the moon and sun. Soon the laughter turned to tears – heavy drops in flat splatters merging quickly as the tears and laughter come faster, soaking my hair and clothes. I joyfully ignore the rain. Soon my nurses come to get me, shaking their heads. They wonder will I get better. I wonder will they let me.

The tower was a post of diligence. I had to look up and down the highway, down the road, rambling, winding away into infinity behind the trees, watching for cars and trucks so the giant dump truck Ukes wouldn't hit anything as they crossed. Twice the size of semis, it was they that hit, no matter the point of impact. I was the one who gave them the yellow light of cautious crossing whenever it was safe. A modicum of responsibility was helpful to my soul. So it is ironic that it is in the tower where it first happened, where my madness first let itself be seen.

Chapter 10

It was a typical night of work: boring. I sat in silence –
perhaps not silence, since I had a radio. Perhaps it wasn't on.
Maybe not. I know I was reading. I also know it was Nietzsche.
My Sister and I.

I went insane. It was the first glance from and into the
abyss I'd received. I put down my book and looked around.
Nothing. As usual. It was 3:00 in the morning. What could
there be? Nothing. A calico cat calendar hung on the wall. I
felt very odd. Everything twisted three degrees. An empty
plastic Subway bag lay in the corner. I started shaking. An
amethyst ring sat on the shelf. Breathing became heavier.
Someone left their cowboy hat on a peg. I felt the complete
and total need to hit something. Black work boots on the floor.
Better, I wanted to throw someone from the tower. Yes. I
really wanted to throw someone from the tower. Anyone. It
didn't matter who. I looked around. I don't understand, but I
had enough reason to know not to hit anything in the metal
tower. The pin-up board. I hit it twice. It almost came down.
I had an idea. I'd write. I'd write.

And so I wrote.

*This was easier to find, since it was in a notebook and not
among the writings he saved on disk. Of course, this made it
much more difficult to reproduce, since I had to interpret his
scribble and transcribe it onto the computer.*

I need to fucking DO something! I can't stand it any longer!
I'm tired of writer's block! I'm tired of having to rely on a bunch
of idiots for my future. I'm tired of having idiots' inane jabber,
mindlessly talking about nothing. I'm extremely fucking tired
of doing what I'm EXPECTED to do. Maybe I don't want to do
what's expected of me. Maybe I want to do what *I* want to do!
I feel ready to explode any minute!!! I am not appreciated for
who and what I am. I am tired of being alone. I am tired of
being a lone voice of truth and morality among a bunch of
brainwashed idiots who have no idea what a fucking principle
is or what a concept is, who cannot recognize evil when it is

pointed out to them. Ignorance is no excuse so long as I yell the truth at the top of my lungs! Does no one think? Does no one know the TRUTH when they see it? Or EVIL? Have we grown so complacent in the evil around us that we no longer care? We need to recognize it, grab it, crush it! The most truthful statement ever made was that a prophet is not appreciated in his own home. I am tired of not being appreciated; I am tired of the ignorance, stupidity, and advocacy of immorality and evil from those that I KNOW know better! I am tired of arguing with those who REFUSE to listen, not because of what is said, so much as it is the person who says it. I am tired of being told I cannot possibly know what I'm talking about, not because of my ignorance, but because of my AGE! Age and wisdom are not necessarily corollaries. There are as many old fools as young sages, if not more. Indeed, it is the pervading foolishness I fight!

Beaten, abused
I find her sitting,
Drinking, eating.
We talk.
I find it easiest to talk
And to listen.
She tells me her stories
As I listen.
We agree to meet again
And again.
We grow close as we talk.
She grows closer
To my heart.
So we hate it when we part.
She finds excuses
To see me.
I must tell her.
She must know!
Or else the depressing darkness
Will pull me deeper within.

Beaten, abused
I know her to be
But still he will not separate from him
For me.

Women must like to be beat
And abused.
To be treated like dirt
To be used as a fucking-post
And little else
To be treated as a thing
And not a person
To be maltreated and mistreated
To be wanted for their tits
And their ass
And whatever hole a dick
Can be shoved in
For whenever a man comes along
Who would love them
As they are
For their mind and spirit
Who would drown them in passion
Rather than lust
To make love
Rather than rut like mindless animals
To treat a woman as a being
Rather than as a convenient hole to fuck
Then this man
A true man
Is alone and lonely
Is not allowed to love

Cured or blessed with an understanding that no one wants or will accept as truth, though the truth is evident; accept as moral, though the morality is evident; accept as rational, though the reason is evident!

Control. None. Can't concentrate. I am going to explode. Can't think. I must, have to get out of here. If I don't get out of Kentucky I'm going to explode!!! I'm tired of the control others have over my life, my happiness! I am tired of not being romantically loved, of my loneliness, of women who don't want a good man, of women who want to be treated like trash! I am tired of being treated like I am insignificant. I am NOT insignificant. If I do not first explode, I will affect the world unlike any before me has! I will fight for freedom and liberty even if none will join me! A few will. A few, a very few have. Stars. Stars and planets are within our grasp if we only reach far enough. Nothing is beyond ME!!! Love? I must change, but get out of here, out of this stagnation! I cannot think straight, where am I going? Why is what I want so difficult to attain? Why can I not accomplish what I want? Is ability so disdained, so hated? Is truth so despised? Is thinking so avoided? Hours. I cannot calm down. I care too much. Why do so many despise greatness? Is it fear? Hatred? Envy? Lust. I am tired of women being treated as things. I am I. I have few (*there is an indecipherable scribble here*): I want someone. Why can't I? The perfect one slipped from me. Did she like her abuse too much? Fine. A fire inside. Burning. Exciting. *It's over*!!! As quickly and suddenly as it began.

During the entire time I wrote, I shook violently. I went insane for an hour. Obviously, I didn't write for an entire hour. It had taken over half an hour to decide to write it out. Before that, I had called Dillon on the C.B. I tried to explain what was happening. He seemed concerned, but brushed it off, though he told me to call him back later. Had he or anyone seen me, I know I would have scared them to death. But when I wrote "It's over," everything snapped to normal. Dillon later called back to make sure I was alright. I was. Afterwards, I mentioned it to no one else.

BOOK 5

It is night.
I know it's night – it's dark.
Those feelings are coming upon me again.
Hello? Who is it?
Come to take me away.
I struggle to stand –
I cannot.
Here they come!
I can feel them!
They're crawling all over!
I struggle to brush them off –
My arms, they will not move.
What is it? What is it?
Get away from me!
I thrash 'round my head
To ward off the bit,
Pain is my only release!
The softness around
Cannot help me, cannot save me!
Help me, save me from this!
The light flickers on,
The strange one walks in,
I finally collapse into sleep.

Chapter 1

That was July 5 – the night I first tasted insanity. In the melancholy moods the nights working as a security guard puts a jilted genius in, I wrote this ten days later:

Signals

She volunteers
To go where I lead.
She tells me all
Her secrets, her hopes, her fears –
More, perhaps, than she would a friend?
Lunch,
Dinner
Three, four
Times a week.
One night she calls
She wants to come over –
An excuse transparent,
Apparent.
She comes, we talk.
Excuse forgotten,
Never realized when she leaves.
Another day,
We part unwillingly
Desperate to find a reason not to part.
I can stand it no longer.
I must tell her.
She answers:
No.

Chapter 2

I fear this is starting to sound like a simple cataloging of things I wrote, connected loosely by events, but I can't think of any other way to say what needs saying. I am my writing, my writing is me. I cannot separate them. To know me, you must know the words I wrote. I am the words.

The poems I wrote at the time are flavored by Sandi's presence, as my life and art still are. One day, I was stationed beside the railroad tracks to flag down the Ukes when a train came. That was an accident no one wanted to see. But trains were few, so I read. At the time, I was reading Nietzsche – *Twilight of the Idols* – and I became enthralled with the beauty of his writing. So enthralled, I walked around in the sunlight, reading the book aloud to myself. I'm sure I looked mad to the men who drove by in their pickups.

Chapter 3

Nietzsche helped to drive me mad – though in truth, I cannot blame him. I wasn't strong enough. I wasn't ready for him. I could only go halfway, and now I reside in the abyss, my eyes locked with its eyes, waiting for release.

As darkness fell, I settled down into the torn, stained orange barco lounger that filled half the guard shack. I was escaping the mosquitoes more than anything; it was an otherwise beautiful night. Sitting, listening to an approaching train, whose presence I could ignore with the fall of night.

A sounding train has rudely come
Upon my train of thought.
And now I find that only some
Seek that which I have sought.

More distractions sounding clear
Through the dark and silent night
Happens on my tender ear
And sends my thoughts to fright.

How can she learn all that I know
With lights and noise around
Putting on, yes, quite a show
So I can't make a sound.

Down we crawl into a hole.
There's no distraction there.
And when we're done, we'll take a stroll,
An intellectual pair.

Chapter 4

Then the job's final insult was made: I was laid off. Our employer had asked the mine for more money so he could give us a raise (at least, that's what he told us), and the mine responded by hiring another company. As though the job itself wasn't insulting enough, the fact that I couldn't keep it, for whatever reason, was yet another bruise to my psyche. So I was laid off, and left without a job for months. Since I still lived with my parents, I was financially unconcerned, so in the intervening months, I worked through the temp services until the company finally called me back to work as a guard at another mine.

I was happy to be back at work, but still unhappy with the job. However, it was not to last long. I had applied and was accepted to be a substitute teacher. Finally, a job that wasn't a complete insult to my intelligence.

Unfortunately, I slipped and mentioned to my immediate supervisor that I had this new job, and was informed within the week by the head of the company that my job was terminated, since they couldn't count on me. At the time, I thought it didn't matter, since I had another job in a few weeks, but maybe it did matter in some small way. When you are as close as I was to the edge, every nudge is dangerous.

Chapter 5

My time off from work – the reason I am in this asylum, an asylum where I am again alone. It was foolish to think I could find love here. Would it have made my mind grow better or worse? At least I wasn't yet in love, not the kind of love that put me here. I've asked around, but I still don't know what happened. A rumor of violence, but only a rumor, though the man involved is no longer here.

Within days of my firing, my mother's brother had a stroke, and her father had another one, too. Her brother was only fifty. I agreed to go with her to visit them in Atlanta. I wanted to be there, though there was nothing I could do. I felt helpless.

Neither was in the hospital, which was fortunate. They had been released before we'd arrived. We stayed at my grandparents' house and visited my uncle. Everyone seemed fine, considering the strokes. Not too much damage, thankfully. Strokes, however, are horrible for one reason more than any other: there's nothing you can do but sit aside and watch helplessly as the mind of your grandfather and uncle are attacked, knowing many more strokes, more the right one, could kill either one. I was helpless, powerless, without control.

On our second night there, after what seemed a normal day, we sat to dinner. As I sat at the dinner table, I slowly stretched my neck.

Suddenly, my grandmother asked, "Are you alright?"

I looked up at her, not realizing anything had happened. The entire world suddenly sharpened, but was somehow not quite right. I looked at her with widened eyes and said, "I . . . I don't know."

She looked at me with strange eyes, concerned, then finished setting the food on the table. As she did, I started rocking back and forth, barely noticeable at first. I was able to eat dinner without it causing problems. But then it worsened. Quickly. Rocking, rocking, rocking. It grew worse. My arms slid up in front of me, my hands clenched. If I tried to stop my body, my arms started moving. I stared at the floor with eyes wide. I felt nothing but fear, and felt I was somehow observing this fear separate from the rest of my body. I became

103

fear. The state I felt myself slipping into scared me as much as the fear I felt. My mother panicked, frightened at my failing state. My grandmother was terrified, too, but suggested they take me to the emergency room.

Chapter 6

I sat in the emergency waiting room, rocking back and forth, scaring everyone in the room. There had been an accident, so I was made to wait for hours. My mother tried to talk to me, asking me questions, making sure I was really there. I could answer her questions, though slowly. She held my hand. She prayed. She cried. She talked with me some more. Finally, they took me to a room to take my blood pressure. The nurse wore an amethyst necklace. A doctor came to see me. He looked in my eyes, trying to see if there was something wrong with the brain, perhaps a tumor. There was nothing. It wasn't physiological. Not on that level. I was slipping away as my brain mistakenly tried to protect the mind and prevent it from being lost, only ensuring that it would be.

I heard the doctor tell my mother there was nothing he could do. Nothing. No control. No control over anything – not even the doctors. Someone had to control something. Someone had to be able to do something. I slid off the bed, turned toward it, and flung it over. The doctor jumped away as my mother screamed. I started flinging things to the floor, trying to avoid visual contact with anyone, to avoid hurting them. I heard the doctor yell something. I was wrestled to the ground, still struggling. I screamed.

Chapter 7

I was sedated and sent into a chemical dream. I cared for nothing. I felt nothing. Nothing was right and I didn't care. Blessed nihilism. But as it wore off, I felt the rocking fear rebuild, a fear that sent me into a reptilian violence, a violence I wouldn't have felt while sane.

I was made to see a psychologist the next day. After questioning my mother and me, he came to the conclusion I had fallen into some kind of deep regression. The rocking was fetal, which meant the mind had gone back to a time it had once felt safe. Need it have gone so far back? Was my mental safety so soon dispersed? The psychologist also said since I was so violent, I shouldn't be sent back home. I should be cared for professionally in a protected place. I was, however, committed closer to home than Atlanta. My mother couldn't have stood it otherwise. I had to be close to home.

Chapter 8

So here I am, receiving my treatments and therapies. Sometimes I feel better. Sometimes I feel the violence creeping in. Some days I know I regress. Today my thoughts are on one thing. I learned what happened.

I have rid myself of violence. For that I am happy. They are far from kind toward violence here, though they are fortunate they removed that man before I learned the truth – I would have turned violent again, if only for a season – only this time, I would have had a very rational reason.

So now I sit in darkness on cloudless noondays in the central lawn waiting for Usas to bare her breasts for me, within me, as she has done for every man on these darkened mornings, waking them to a new day, waking them to life. Why has she forsaken me for her sister for so long, leaving me in twilight's perpetual darkness while she dutifully wakens the rest of mankind? Why has she allowed Ratri permanent sanctuary, a permanent residence within my soul? What has Usas done for me of late that I should be thankful for the dawn? Her dawns have not risen in me for years, yet she still expects devotion? I will see to her when she sees to my dawns! But Usas' absence at least no longer drives me mad with violence. For that I am thankful. Perhaps that is a glimmer of her light? No? The dawn draws down deep deliverance of dreary dark devils damaged, savaged, ravaged round rapid recourses of repeating reasons we see inside our inner selves. Where were we when we wanted our lives to turn to one? My mind melted, mellowed in mire made morose. And yet I looked, lost in love, laboring lightly through too loose light lingering in love. Years yet withstanding, wandering lost in yellow yearnings of youth, I could, should, would in good faith find for free a focused frame of mind. Fine.

We wandered in lost loneliness, our lives we now have found a mess. Unfocused lives we now address and find ourselves, our souls depressed, unable to stand the evil world set around us. Beautiful souls killing themselves for the evil perpetuated on them again in a place where they should have been safe. She is dead, my little loved one here in the asylum, and my soul has died a little more for her.

Chapter 9

I was driven mad by love, by my inability to control the things I felt I should. I couldn't control the world, so I left it. I wouldn't be loved, so I refused to be a part of the world.

Unloved, I lie in pain, agony, tears drown cheeks in eye's founts – of youth's pain I know more than any cares, more than Erzulie Ge-Rouge. I lie unloved in the way I need, I lie unloved, with dying seed of my soul wallowing in the filth of this world that destroys those who need to love, who have such a love to give as I have had in this life. Why? Why! Why must I lie unloved, literally laboring for the little life left living inside my broken body – body broken by battered soul? Why must the greatest souls be denied the love we know? Unallowed to depart or impart it to a woman worthy of our love. I haven't known a woman worthy of my love – those I thought were at first have proven me wrong. Is there none on this earth for me, worthy of the love I need to give, ready for the love I wish to give, wanting the love I have to give? I, who have such love to impart, I who must remain unloved, I, I am destroyed by this unloved, unloving world because none will love me. The madness of love is the greatest of heaven's blessings? Yes, Plato, it is, unless that love is unreturned. Then it becomes mere madness. The lover, the madman, and the poet are all of one soul in me.

Unwanted, I writhe in pain, agony. Tears can come no more – they are replaced by the blinding ache – filling me until I feel the nausea rising in my throat. The inner screams ripping through, threaten to form on my tongue and lips. A need to be wanted, I want to be needed, I need to be loved, I'd love to be wanted. Where want whispers warily while waiting for ...what? Why can't I fly my need so high 'til I find the one I need, who needs of me, lest we die? I die a death a minute when I find I am unwanted. I cannot win without the love I know I need. I find I cry, I cannot finish, what I know my love cannot diminish, lest I make my forearms bleed. Crying, crying I live unloved, dying, dying, I cannot live unwanted.

Unappreciated for all I do, my love, my pain, art, help, knowledge too. The help I give, no one cares, the love I need,

109

the soul it bares. I will not go the rest of my life unappreciated as the destructive, hateful, stupid world does this to the rest of those who are great in spirit. Killing greatness, great minds, great spirits, great hearts, great loves, great needs, I will not stand any longer for it! We must kill it lest it kills us in the mindless malevolent mediocrity that clearly destroys only the gallant, the greatness in good men. I will not let it destroy me because I go through life unappreciated! Never! Never! God, no, never!

And yet I lie in darkness' streets,
I feel my soul is not complete –
It lies, it writes, it cannot help
But fall in gutters, drainpipes trelp
Garxy nixle forsy gelp
Ickse molby whorgral belp

Where do I lie, how can I know?
In gutters, drainpipes full of snow.
Drizzle, fizzle, bagpipes glow,
Forget your love's ass, it's too slow.
Hear drum's harmony, panflute's beat
While licking batwings, good to eat.

One wonders why wings wrap around
Pussy's whiskers cannot be found,
Insects eaten, sweet lime ground,
Up we find the sky lay down.
Myxl figures know in time,
We killed and ate the sperm whale mime.
This life we know is such a treat,
We cut our throats and take a seat.

Chapter 10

I sit here Sandi and die for you. I lie here Sandi and die for you, for all the pain you brought to me. I walk these halls and die for you. I rock here now and die for you. My life is death, I die for you. I sigh, I cry, I lie, I die, I wonder why, and yet I cannot do enough no matter what I try for you. Will you understand what you've done, the pain you've brought, the whips you've brandished? Will you even try? By the love I feel for you still – after all this now I wonder why – I swear in darkness I will not die no matter if the pain and darkness draws a cry. I will not die, I cannot die, I will not, shall not die for you. Although I have lost both you and the lovely little girl that brought my mind some comfort while I was here, I will not die for you or her.

I have found my madness better focused in my writing. Perhaps Plato was right here – when it comes to art, perhaps the sane man is indeed nowhere at all when he enters into rivalry with the madman. I was nowhere near this lyrically without my madness. Since I started writing, I have failed to find my fear so dreadful, my pain is now more bearable. I find I no longer need my violent outbursts. I thank you for lending me your eye. That, perhaps, is what I've needed: someone to listen, someone to read me, someone to understand. That's why I've told you this story. We all wish to drink from Govannon's brew, we poets, we writers, we creators. It is why we do what we do. We know our bodies can't be immortal, but we hope our minds will be, through you.

Fin

About the Author...

Like Patric, Troy Camplin has a B.A. in recombinant gene technology from Western Kentucky University; unlike Patric, he also has a M.A. in English from the University of Southern Mississippi and a Ph.D. in the humanities from UT-Dallas. In addition to short fiction and novellas, Camplin also writes poetry and plays. One play, "Almost Ithacad," won first prize at the Cyberfest playwriting festival. In addition to his literary writing, Camplin has also published popular pieces on culture and society, particularly on education, and scholarly works on spontaneous order theory. He currently resides in Richardson, TX with his wife and three children.

Made in the USA
Columbia, SC
11 April 2019